The tightening circle
of lizard bodies
pulled back slightly,
and Lewis shuddered
with relief.

They believed him. Maybe they would let him
go . . . but then a shadow fell between the crowd
of salamanders and the greenish glow on the
wall—a shadow taller and more massive than any
of the lizards. The salamanders cringed, their
bellies flat against the ground.

"Bring him," a deep voice said from just
beyond Lewis's sight.

Sign on for myth and magic with the

VOYAGE OF THE BASSET

Voyage of the Basset

Fire Bird

BY
Mary Frances Zambreno

Random House 🏠 New York

This book is for my brother, John Zambreno,
who gave me the computer to write it on.
Thank you again, John.

Copyright © 2001 by James C. Christensen and The Greenwich Workshop®,
Inc. All rights reserved under International and Pan-American Copyright
Conventions. Published in the United States by Random House, Inc.,
New York, and simultaneously in Canada by Random House of Canada
Limited, Toronto. Based on *Voyage of the Basset* by James C. Christensen,
a Greenwich Workshop book published by Artisan, 1996, and licensed by
The Greenwich Workshop®, Inc.

www.randomhouse.com/kids

Library of Congress Cataloging-in-Publication Data
Zambreno, Mary Frances.
Fire bird / by Mary Frances Zambreno. p. cm. — (Voyage of the Basset ; 5)
SUMMARY: Thirteen-year-old Emily, her blind engineer father, and a boy
from their English village sail aboard the magic ship *Basset* to an island of
mythical animals, where they use faith and imagination to try to restore a
legendary lighthouse tower.
ISBN 0-375-81109-5 [1. Magic—Fiction. 2. Lighthouses—Fiction.
3. Mythology, Classical—Fiction. 4. Animals, Mythical—Fiction.
5. Faith—Fiction. 6. Imagination—Fiction.
7. Fathers and daughters—Fiction.] I. Title. II. Series.
PZ7.Z2545 Fi 2001 [Fic]—dc21 00-46029

Printed in the United States of America June 2001 10 9 8 7 6 5 4 3 2 1

RANDOM HOUSE and colophon are registered trademarks of Random House, Inc.

Cover illustration by James C. Christensen.

CONTENTS

VOYAGE

OF THE BASSET

FIRE BIRD

1
STRANGE SHIP IN THE HARBOR

It was raining that mid-May morning in Cornwall as thirteen-year-old Emily Alexander came down the front stairs of the drafty old house known as Petherick Place. Through the long windows in the front hall, she could see sky as gray as lead. But then, it was almost always raining and gloomy in the little fishing village of Aldestow, though the Cornish peninsula itself boasted of being the southernmost tip of England. It had been over a year since she and her father had moved into the house that had once belonged to her mother's family, and Emily could count the sunny days they'd seen on the fingers of one hand.

And not need my thumb, she thought sourly, walking into the breakfast room. One thing Petherick Place had was rooms—a formal dining room as well as a breakfast room, a ballroom, a dilapidated library that her father used as his study—even a billiards room, though the table was long gone. *At least the fire is lit. Bless Mrs. Giffey.*

"Good morning, Papa," she said sedately, taking her place at her father's right. James Alexander sat at the head of the table, as usual, while Thomas Bentham—his secretary—had copped the chair closest to the fire. Also as usual. "Thomas."

"Good morning, my dear," her father answered, almost cheerful for such a dismal day. Being blind, he hadn't seen her come in, but the expression on his scarred face warmed at the sound of her voice. From Thomas she got only a nod and a surly grunt—Thomas was much too lazy to say hello to someone as unimportant as his employer's daughter. "Thomas, I'm expecting a new design proposal from the Lighthouse Authority sometime this week—perhaps as early as today's mail. You'll want to go down to the harbor to fetch it."

"It's too soon," Thomas grumbled, sounding startled and a little sulky. A round, sleek young man, he was technically an apprentice engineer as well as James Alexander's corresponding secretary, but he hated running errands into the village. "The Authority won't have anything for us yet. *If* they plan to send us anything at all this season."

Emily could have kicked Thomas right in his plump shins. She would have, too, if he hadn't been sitting so far away. *Why does he always have to be so negative?* she thought angrily. It was what she despised most about her father's secretary— even more than his laziness. *He knew Papa was blind when he came here. Of course the Lighthouse Authority will send a new proposal! They had a commission for Papa last year, didn't they? Not much of a one, but that <u>was</u> right after the accident. He's still the most experienced consultant they have.*

Only a year before, James Alexander had been more than a fine mathematician and consulting engineer. He had been one of England's most promising *lighthouse* engineers, a specialist in designing and building the wave-swept towers that were changing the coastline of Great Britain forever and might well change the whole world one day. Then an oil lamp had exploded while he was working on it, leaving him with a jaggedly scarred face and sightless, empty eyes—and a sadly diminished future.

None of which mattered just at the moment.

"I'll go to the harbor for you, Papa," Emily said quickly, before Thomas could say another word. "I was intending to go down to the market right after breakfast, anyway."

"Well, if you're sure it's no trouble . . . dress warmly." He always said that when she went down to the harbor—it was catching cold after a rainstorm that had killed her mother two years ago—but Emily could tell he was relieved. He hated having to bully Thomas almost as much as Thomas hated running errands. "The specifications should be boxed and waiting for you at the receiving office. Make certain that Sweeney gives you the whole package."

Thomas cast her a look of burning dislike—if there was a package waiting at the receiving office, then he might actually have to do some *work* that afternoon—but she ignored him, concentrating instead on pouring milk on her father's porridge so that he wouldn't have to do it for himself. Papa did so dislike spilling things, but sometimes he couldn't help it, now that he couldn't see. There were so many things he couldn't do for himself anymore . . . like running down to the village, instead relying on his reluctant secretary. Or his daughter.

Mama was right, Emily thought, spooning sugar onto her own cereal. *He needs me so much.* She'd promised her mother she'd take care of him, and Emily meant to keep that promise. Of course, Marian Petherick hadn't known then that her husband would be blinded—couldn't have known about the accident, still a year in the future. But that didn't change the situation, so far as her daughter was concerned. *Blast Thomas, anyway. I hope the Lighthouse Authority has sent lots of new work.* The fees would certainly be welcome, too. Petherick Place could use a new roof sometime before the turn of the nineteenth century. . . .

After breakfast Emily had a few words with Mrs. Giffey, the woman who came in daily from the village to do the cooking and washing up, and then she fetched her cloak. The heavy rain of the morning had turned into a light, chilly mist, but the wind had picked up enough to cut right to the bone. Emily shivered as she pulled her hood more tightly around her head.

Just as well it's me running errands and not Thomas, at that, she thought, starting down the long hill to the village—"going down-along," as the people of Aldestow would say. Thomas tended to speak to the villagers very, very slowly, as if they were either simple or hard of hearing. The last time he'd had to go down to the harbor, he'd managed to offend the grocer's wife, the local minister, and three of the village's leading tradesmen—all without even trying. Emily couldn't blame them for being insulted. *I thought he was going to be run out of town on a rail, and what would Papa have done then?*

Much as she disliked Thomas, she had to admit that her father had been lucky to find him. There weren't many engineering students willing to move to the wilds of Cornwall to work with a blind man, especially not for the salary James Alexander could offer.

Safely away from her father's keen ears, Emily sighed. Fancy having to be grateful for Thomas Bentham! Well, needs must, she supposed. In the middle distance, she could see the gray water of the river, and beyond that the even drearier gray of the harbor. The prospect might have been pleasant to other eyes, she knew. Aldestow was a typically quaint Cornish fishing village, the sort that artists from all over England visited to paint landscapes of, rejoicing loudly in its unspoiled beauty. (No one had mentioned, in Emily's hearing at least, that "unspoiled" usually meant inconvenient and uncomfortable as well.) It had whitewashed, thatched cottages with hedged flower gardens, and a picturesque harbor on the mouth of the River Camel that was mentioned in all of the guidebooks. The village church, St. Piran's, had been built in the fourteenth century and was largely unchanged since that time, while the mountains of Rough Tor and Redruth lifted in yellow furze–covered majesty across the inland horizon. The view in that direction was pretty enough, she supposed. If you liked mountains.

As for the famous harbor itself . . . well, it was lined with local fishing boats jostling for mooring, their gaily striped sails adding color to the grayness of the water and the even more dismal grayness of the overcast sky, while the occasional pleasure boat or ocean clipper offered variety. The harbor mouth was bottomed with golden sand, treacherous to sail but undeniably lovely when the weather was clear. Emily could take it or leave it.

For the most part, she preferred to leave it. Unfortunately, she didn't always have a choice. Like today.

In spite of the rain, the Aldestow Harbor shipyards were crowded with men waiting for work, and the ropewalks were busier than usual, turning out lines of twisted hemp for the local trade. The fishing fleet was in, it appeared. Emily quickened her step, heading for the receiving office on the main wharf.

"Hello, Mr. Sweeney," she said, shaking the water off her cloak in the doorway.

"Hello, Miss Emily," the agent said cordially enough. He was wearing a green eyeshade and an apron, as befit his dual role of clerk and village grocer. "What can I do for you this fine day?"

Fine day? It's been raining buckets, she thought, amused. *He's probably just glad to see me and not Thomas.* But of course she couldn't say that. Instead, she asked: "Are there any packages for Petherick Place today?"

"I don't think so." Fastidiously, he wiped his hands on his none-too-clean apron and looked around the room, as if there might be a box hiding in the corner. "No, no packages for the Place."

Oh, no! "Are you certain? My father has been expecting something from Edinburgh, and it should be here by now."

"No package as I know of, miss," he told her, round face wrinkling in concern. He was a nice man, for the most part. "Nor letters, either, and the mail ship's been and gone."

"But—" Just in time, she cut off the harsh words that trembled on her tongue. It wasn't the agent's fault, after all. *Thomas was right,* she thought—*forced* herself to think. *It's too soon. . . . It <u>must</u> be too soon.* The other possibility—that there would be no package from Edinburgh—was something she refused to consider. "Thank you, Mr. Sweeney. If a box comes for Petherick Place later today, will you send word?"

"I will," he said, nodding. "'Tis low tide a'ready, though."

He meant that new arrivals were unlikely,

Emily knew. Aldestow Harbor was dangerous enough to enter at high tide; no sane ship's master would risk the treacherous sea-sands when the tide was out.

Papa will be so disappointed, she thought as she left the receiving office. Outside, it was still raining—misting, rather—but the thought of James Alexander's disappointment made Emily disinclined to hurry home. What was there to go home for, in any case? Slowly, she started walking along the wharf, trying to think of something that would lift her father's spirits. *How will I ever tell him? Maybe—maybe if I—if we write to the Lighthouse Authority again tomorrow, to ask . . .*

So intent was she on her plans that she didn't notice the little crowd on the north pier until she'd almost run into it: village boys, mostly. What were they all looking at? Curious, she craned her neck, trying to see over the heads blocking her view.

"She'll never make it," said one of them, indistinguishable in the crowd. He seemed more pleased than not. "Her master's a proper gate bufflehead, tryin' to bring her into Aldestow Harbor at low tide."

"Aye, she'll hang up on Doom Bar fer sure," said another. Emily recognized Gloomy Gus Colcannon, who sometimes did heavy work in the garden up at Petherick Place and who never saw the good side of anything. "Bet her skipper scritches like a whitneck when she runs aground."

Meaning "screams like a weasel," though Emily hadn't a clue what a screaming weasel sounded like. She'd certainly never heard one. Then she saw what they were looking at, the little ship tacking so bravely into the harbor's mouth, and forgot everything else. *Oh, what a lovely little ship! But surely—the tide—it's so dangerous!*

She *was* a lovely ship, all curves and bows and curlicues, with a bright gold-and-blue banner that fluttered gaily against the dullness of the sky. HMS—HMS *Basic?* No, the HMS *Basset.* Her railings and decks were trimly elegant, the wood warm with polish, and her brasses glittered even under the cloudy sky; she looked more like a child's toy than an oceangoing vessel, but she must have come from very far away to be daring enough to enter *this* harbor at low tide. Any local ship would have known the risks and waited.

The blue-and-gold banner whipped with the offshore breeze. Squinting, Emily tried to read it. _Credo_ ... _Credendo_ ... _Credendo vides._ *That's Latin,* she thought. Something about seeing and believing. *I'll have to ask Papa.*

If the ship made port safely, she'd ask. Otherwise—well, James Alexander had enough to depress him without being troubled by the misfortunes of others.

Be careful, HMS Basset, Emily prayed, her heart in her mouth. A ship that ran aground while sailing into Aldestow Harbor was a ship in danger of breaking up; sometimes the crew was able to get off before she foundered, and sometimes not. It all depended. *Oh, do be careful! If you aren't, then the wreckers will have you. . . .*

Almost as if the ship could hear, she slowed, edging forward an inch at a time. The figures of her crew, tiny in the distance, raced up and down her masts, re-rigging the sails. Port for a ship's length or two—then slightly starboard—then, incredibly, back a bit—Emily hadn't a clue how that was accomplished, but she wasn't a sailor—and then *forward,* strongly, under full sail, until finally the elegant prow was pointed straight ahead into the harbor, sailing freely as the ship made for mooring.

"Hurrah!" Emily cheered, clapping her hands delightedly. "She's safe! She made it!"

"More's the pity," grumbled the first boy who had spoken. He was a short, stocky lad about her own age with rumpled brown hair and a square face, wearing a rough tweed jacket that looked as though it had been cut down from two sizes too large for him. "Thought the mermaid's curse had another one, eh, boys?"

The crowd muttered its agreement.

The mermaid's curse . . . Emily couldn't help staring. "What do you mean?"

"Dun't ye know the tale?" the boy said. He did seem vaguely familiar, now that she had a chance to look at him closely—someone she'd seen around the village, most likely, or had had pointed out to her by Mrs. Giffey. "'Twas a wounded mermaid who cursed Aldestow Harbor so the harbor mouth is choked with drifting sea-sand. She was angry, it's said, at the fisherman who tried to capture her in his net. . . ."

He lowered his voice dramatically at the last words, eyes gleaming with expectant relish. Did he think she'd be afraid? Of what?

"I don't believe in mermaids," Emily told him primly—and then stopped as another thought occurred to her. "You mean you *wanted* that little ship to run aground?"

The brown-haired boy shrugged. "Not to say *wanted*. But if she did, there'd be some fine salvage to be had, fer sure."

Salvage. Of course. On the rocky coast of Cornwall, scavenging cargo from wrecked ships was a tradition. But most people weren't quite so open about wishing for disaster, even so.

"That's awful," Emily said in disgust, and then—finally—realized who she was talking to.

"Oh, I know who you are now. You're that Lewis Trelawny boy."

"I am," he said, looking her up and down belligerently. "What's it to you?"

"Only that it's the sort of remark I would have expected from *you*," she said, sniffing. Mrs. Giffey had told her the story, in one of her gossipy moods: about how a local man, Jack Trelawny, had been taken for stealing from a stranded but seaworthy ship—rather than just salvaging cargo from a wrecked one—and transported to Australia. According to Mrs. Giffey, he'd have left his wife and young son to the charity of the village if it weren't for the man's own brother taking them in. At the time, Emily hadn't thought much about it, beyond feeling vaguely sorry for the criminal's family, but now . . . "From the son of a thieving wrecker, that is."

The boy flushed. "My dad is not a thief!"

Well, maybe she shouldn't have said it, but it *was* true. "He isn't? Then I suppose he emigrated to Australia on purpose, just because he liked the climate."

That sally won a few snickers of approval from the crowd.

"Aye, Cousin Lewis, ye never thought o' that, did ye," said a big black-haired lout—a Trelawny cousin of some sort, by the resemblance between him and the shorter, stockier Lewis. Emily didn't appreciate the support, but she couldn't stop him speaking up, either. "Liked the climate, haw."

Lewis scowled, glaring at Emily. "Now see here, girl, just because my dad made a mistake dun't mean—why, I know you!" A note of pleased discovery. "You're that Alexander girl from up at the Place—the poor blind man's daughter!"

At his words, Emily froze. No one talked slightingly of her father's blindness. *No* one.

"I—beg—your—pardon," she said, biting off each word very precisely.

· "Yah! Go ahead an' beg," Lewis said, jeering. He glanced sideways, as if gauging the reaction of his audience. "If it weren't for the rich family o' yer dead mother, yer dad'd be out begging in the streets with the other cripples. Right, cousins?"

Laughter, harsh and horrible, as the other boys took his meaning. Pokes and prods of acknowledgment, a few sneers of "Well said, young Lewis!" "Tell 'er, Coz!" Were they all Trelawnys or Trelawny kin? So it seemed. She knew she was being foolish, but she couldn't help it. How dared they? How *dared* they laugh at her father, and at all the pain and suffering and loss since the accident?

"My father is a consulting engineer," she said furiously, stepping forward to confront Lewis

directly. It gave her great satisfaction to realize
that she was at least two inches taller than he
was—tall enough to make him look up at her,
which he didn't seem to like at all. He scowled,
but met her glare for glare. "A *lighthouse* engineer. Why, he trained under the great Robert
Stevenson, who built the Bell Rock Light!"

"But he's blind," someone in the crowd
protested. Emily was too intent on Lewis to
bother looking around to see who it was.

"Oh, I don't think Robert Stevenson is blind,"
she said judiciously. "Do you? Of course, he's
been dead for several years. . . ."

The fickle audience thought that was very
funny; Lewis didn't.

"Lighthouses take food out of the mouths of
honest men's families," he said, sneering the
words. "Time was, a man could get a good living
off salvage anywhere on the coast, from Piran's
Point to Land's End. Not anymore—not since
they built the Wolf's Head Light!"

Emily froze. Of all the ridiculous, small-
minded, petty things she'd ever heard any
Aldestow villager say, this was by far the worst.
To hear anyone, even a stupid boy—the son of a
convicted criminal—mock her own father's pro-
fession . . . it was more than she could bear.

"Lighthouses save lives, my father says," she
told him, as coldly angry as she'd ever been in

her life. "They prevent wrecks. They're—they're *good* things, benefits to humanity."

"They're a waste of time an' money," Lewis answered her, scowling ferociously. "*My* dad says they're against nature—"

"You—you—" She gulped, tried again. "How dare you—"

"Oh, I dare plenty, blind man's girl," he said, grinning in triumph. "I'm just a *thievin' wrecker's son,* remember?"

No, I shouldn't have said that, she realized distantly. *Even if it's true.*

But that didn't matter anymore. Tears choked her, but she would not cry in front of this—this *boy*! Her fists clenched, and almost before she realized what she was doing, she lashed out, striking Lewis full in the face. Caught by surprise, he staggered backward and hit the wharf with a solid *thump*.

"And *I* am an engineer's daughter," she said. "Wrecker's boy."

Turning on her heel, she strode off, leaving him sitting there, his mouth open in shock and his left eye already turning purple.

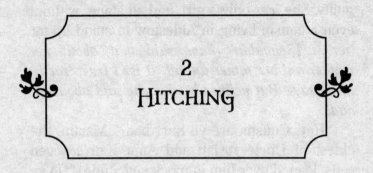

2
HITCHING

Lewis Trelawny sat on his rump, staring after Miss Emily Alexander and feeling as though the whole world had just turned upside down. She'd hit him! Tenderly, he felt the left side of his face—swelling already. He'd been decked by a girl. Probably he'd have a black eye, too, by tomorrow. What Mum would say when she saw . . . and Uncle Josiah! It wasn't to be thought of.

She's a girl, he thought, aggrieved. *Girls shouldn't ought to be hitting people an' blacking their eyes. 'Tis not proper!* What had she to be so angry about? He was only saying what everyone knew about lighthouses—what his dad had always told him. But he'd seen the glitter of tears on Emily Alexander's face as she had stormed away, and the realization that he'd made her cry left him feeling somehow both resentful and guilty. She *was* only a girl, and all alone, without even a cousin living in Aldestow to stand up for her. . . . *I shouldn't have said that about her mother an' her father an' all. It isn't true, 'zactly, Mum says. But neither is what she said about my dad!*

"Hey, Cousin, are ye hurt bad?" Martin, the eldest of Uncle Josiah and Aunt Kate's seven sons, leaned over him in mock solicitude. "Do ye need a hand up?"

Uh-oh. Abruptly, Lewis was recalled to the full horror of the situation. Never mind Mum or Uncle Josiah—his cousins had seen the girl knock him down. He was in for it now, and no mistake.

"His eye's swellin'," Denny, the next oldest, sniggered. The rest of the pack was circling, scenting blood. "Poor Lewis, gettin' his eye blacked by a *girl*."

"Poor Lewis," Zachary, the fourth-from-youngest, echoed, grinning maliciously. "Felled like a Bodmin wrestler on fair day, and by a little *maid*! Best get home to yer mum, baby boy, an' let her cry over ye. . . ."

Since Zach was scarcely a year older than Lewis, if considerably larger, this was an insult not to be endured.

"You take that back," Lewis snarled, struggling to his feet. Zach had no right to talk about his mother—no more than Emily Alexander had had to speak scornfully of his father. "I'm old enough to thump you, so I am!"

"But not old enough to duck from a girl," Denny chortled. He poked Martin in the ribs. "Eh, Mart?"

"She took me by surprise, is all," Lewis said, knowing he was wasting his time. Still, the defense had to be made, for future reference if for nothing else. Otherwise, his life wouldn't be worth living. "Besides, would you have me hit a *girl*? Think what Uncle Josiah would say if he heard I'd hit Miss Alexander of Petherick Place—or worse, what Aunt Kate would say!"

That gave them a brief moment of pause: every one of the Trelawny brood knew better than to offer back talk to their mother, who had as heavy a hand for slapping faces as she did a light touch for pastry. But since Aunt Kate was off home and not actually on the wharf, it was only a moment.

"Didn't seem to me that you had much chance to hit back, sprat," Zachary drawled superciliously. He winked at his brothers. "Eh, lads? You just sat on your backside gawpin', far as I could tell. Could be ye was afraid of gettin' hit again?"

"I was not," Lewis said, stepping up defiantly.

His palms were sweating, and there was a sinking feeling in the pit of his stomach. He didn't *want* to fight Zach, especially not in front of all the rest of his cousins, but he couldn't back down now. "I'm not afraid of anything—especially not your big mouth!"

That, of course, was the final challenge. Zachary shoved him. Staggering, Lewis fought to regain his balance, found his footing—and sprang, knocking the bigger boy down. The others scattered, shouting.

"A hitch! A hitch! Lewis an' Zach're having a hitch! Come an' see!"

Rolling over and over on the boards, Lewis came up hard against a post and gasped as Zach viciously bent his arm backward. Much more of that and he'd have a dislocated elbow! Zachary was stronger than he was as well as larger— Lewis had to get him pinned, and fast. Lifting a knee, he lashed out, catching his opponent in the breadbasket.

"Oww!" Zach yelled, doubling up on the ground. "You little—"

Rolling again, one wrestling over the other, but they were too close to the water to roll far, and this time Lewis came out on top. Sitting on his cousin's chest, he grabbed for the older boy's ears and twisted. Zachary had such nice big ears—useful as handles, they were, if not especially clean.

"Give over," he gasped, leaning into the twist with all his strength. "Give over, or I'll rip yer ears off an' feed 'em to ye!"

"*Niaouh!* No! *Agh!*"

"Zachary!" A voice like thunder on high, rolling across the wharf. Lewis jerked upright, suddenly more frightened than he'd been when he'd realized he'd have to fight. "Lewis! Cease this unseemly brawl at once!"

Instantly, Lewis let go of his cousin's jacket and sat up. "Uncle Josiah! I thought—"

"You thought I was out with the nets on the *Maid o' Moidart* and would not see this disgraceful display," his uncle said grimly, naming the fishing boat that provided the whole family with its living. "Well, I was not, and I have seen. Stand up, both of you. I want a clear look at you."

Abashed, Lewis clambered off his cousin's prone form and stood. His arm and his shoulder hurt worse than his eye—well, that was as it should be. He offered a helping hand to Zach, who rejected it angrily.

"He started it, Dad! He always—"

"Be quiet!" Josiah Trelawny was a tall, broad man with heavy fists, trained in a hard school. Zach went as still as a stone. Lewis could almost have pitied him. Almost. "Lewis. *Did* you strike the first blow?"

Lewis debated briefly. Tell his uncle about his spat with Emily Alexander? No, not if he could possibly help it. Uncle Josiah really wouldn't like it that Miss Emily Alexander of Petherick Place had been even slightly involved in this little brawl. A quick sidelong glance at Zachary showed that his cousin agreed with him; the other boy's eyes were rolling whitely. "Yes. Yes, I did, Uncle."

Zach breathed out, all too obviously relieved. Lewis did his best to ignore him. *Idiot. He'll give the game away.*

"Very well." His uncle exhibited neither disappointment nor satisfaction. "You are my nephew, and I stand as father to you, as to my own boys, and have a father's duty to correct you. For the moment, you will go to the market, where your mother went this morning. Doubtless she will appreciate a hand in carrying home her purchases. When you see her, you will explain to her that you are to be sent to bed without dinner tonight, and why. This evening, I will see you in the woodshed."

Lewis winced. Stand as a father, did Uncle Jos say? His own father had never hit so hard. And to receive another switching so soon after the last— he'd be lucky if he could sit down before midsummer. But there was no help for it; he had to take his punishment like a man, or it would go even worse for him.

"Yes, Uncle," he said, head properly and humbly lowered.

Zach grinned meanly at his cousin's discomfiture. Too soon, as it happened. His father turned cold eyes on him.

"Zachary, the nets on the *Maid o' Moidart* require mending. You are old enough to take on that responsibility on your own, I believe. If you work hard the rest of today and all day tomorrow, you should be able to finish by the day after that."

The grin vanished. "But, Dad—I was goin' to Bodmin Fair tomorrow, to Barry Fish. . . ."

"You will not," Uncle Josiah said. "Dennis and Martin will carry today's catch to the fishmonger. It's none so large that the two of them cannot manage." The edge in his voice made Lewis glance up alertly, and he saw appalled understanding spread among his cousins at the same time. Fishing had been bad all season. If Uncle Jos had had to pull up his nets and come in early, no wonder he was in a foul mood. And in a foul mood, Josiah Trelawny was more dangerous than a northwest gale. "Now—away with you! All of you! And let's have no more o' this fightin' in public!"

A cloud of boys scattered instantly to the four

winds: no one argued with Josiah Trelawny when he took that tone. Least of all his no-good brother's no-good boy, living on charity and scarcely worth the food it took to feed him.

Head bent, Lewis started to trudge back into town alone. No more fighting in public, eh? Did that mean it was all right to fight in private? Sometimes adult logic escaped him, especially his uncle's. At least he'd managed to avoid mentioning Emily Alexander, which was something. . . . Lewis grimaced. He'd had his eye blacked by a miss, not just a girl. Maybe his cousins would conveniently forget about that in their anxiety to keep it from their father—but he doubted it. They'd just be careful not to bring it up in front of Uncle Jos or Aunt Kate, was all.

Well, at least Mum would be pleased to see him—until she saw his eye. Frowning, he braced himself for squalls. Mum wouldn't like it that he and Zach had been hitchin'. . . .

Alice Trelawny was coming out of the green-grocer's when he went up to her, a heavy market basket over her arm. Her thin face lighted with a transforming smile when she saw her son.

"Lewis, love! I wasn't expectin' you!"

"Uncle Jos sent me," he told her. Best to get over heavy ground quickly. And no sense in mentioning Emily Alexander to Mum, either—not so long as the others kept their mouths shut. "He caught Zach an' me fightin' and says I'm to be punished with no dinner tonight. An' the woodshed."

"Oh, Lew, not again," she mourned, pushing a strand of her fine brown hair back under her cap. She was so pale, his mum, not sturdy and brown like Aunt Kate. Sometimes he thought that half of her had gone to Australia with his dad. "You must not, love. We owe yer uncle an' aunt so much!"

A warm place to sleep and food to fill their bellies, that was what they owed Uncle Jos and Aunt Kate—neither of which would have been necessary if his father hadn't been transported.

"I know," he said gruffly, reaching for the market basket. "But that's no reason to work you like a three-legged dog herding sheep. Here, let me carry that. It's too heavy for you."

"I dun't mind a few little chores," she said, as she always did, but she sighed with relief as he lifted the weight from her arm. "Not when we've so much to be grateful for. . . ."

"Grateful!" Unable to stop himself, he snorted in derision. "You do all the marketin' and most all o' the laundry an' sewin'—you cook and clean and scrub till yer fingers are bloody, an' all Aunt Kate does is bake and gossip with the neighbors about what a charge we are on the house. If Dad could see—"

"That's enough," Alice Trelawny said sharply.

"Yer father *isn't* here to see, and whose fault is that, may I ask? Jack Trelawny broke the law. It's why he was transported and left us here to fend for ourselves on your uncle's charity."

"Dad didn't know there was anyone left alive on the *Carlisle!*" Lewis burst out angrily. Emily Alexander had called his father a thief, but he wasn't. He *wasn't!* "He thought he had fair right o' wreck, or he'd never have gone near that ship!"

"But there *was* someone left alive," his mother told him firmly, answering him as she had too many times before. "Two men and a dog, brought safe to shore *after* yer father was seen salvaging cargo. He should have known better, and he's paid for it, poor man. As have we."

The pain in her voice made Lewis flinch—made him want to hit someone, preferably his cousin Zachary. That was the heart of the matter, the single mistake that had cost Jack Trelawny his freedom and his family: an abandoned vessel might be counted as wrecked and legally salvaged, but the *Carlisle* hadn't been abandoned. Not quite. "I'm sorry, Mum. I didn't mean—"

"I know you didn't," she said, sighing and shaking her head. "Never mind, love. But when I think of yer father, an' his wreckin'—'tis so *dangerous,* Lew. If it isn't the law, 'tis the wind and waves, sweepin' men to their doom. And fer what? A few shillin's' worth o' salvage? 'Tis not worth it."

"Good money in wreckin'," he muttered, scuffing one toe in the dirt path. "If only you'd let me—"

"Lewis." She stopped, her face serious as well as sad. "I've told you and told you. Promise me you'll never go wreckin' like yer father."

The same old demand—the same old fear. Wrecking wasn't *that* dangerous. And he was the man of the house now. Couldn't she understand? "Mum, I wouldn't be lost. I'd be careful."

"Yer father was careful, and he ended up in Australia." Her mouth set in a thin, stubborn line that he knew only too well. "Promise me, Lewis. Promise me you won't go wreckin' like yer dad. Promise!"

As if an Aldestow boy had any real chance at ready money except in wrecking . . .

But he couldn't start the old argument again. Not now. Alice Trelawny had faced enough loss and pain in her life; her son couldn't let himself add to it. Lewis sighed, surrendering.

"I won't, Mum," he said, repeating the words he'd already said more times than he could count. "I promise."

"Then we'll say no more about it." She tousled his hair lightly. "I dun't know as I can blame you fer speakin' up fer yer dad, at that. You're his son, when all's said, an' I wouldn't have ye different. Now come home-along with me an' wash yer face. I'll get you a bit o' beef to put on that eye."

Home-along, he thought bitterly. As if his uncle and aunt's house could ever truly be home for either of them. Even the prospect of the woodshed didn't sting so sharply as that. Jack Trelawny had only been trying to provide for his family when he'd been taken by the law. He'd done nothing wrong—not really wrong. His son knew it and his wife knew it, or would if only she'd stop trying to keep Lewis from following in his father's footsteps. *If only we'd been able to go with Dad to Australia!*

A new life in a distant land. . . . It wouldn't have been so bad. But there hadn't been enough money for two more passages, even in steerage, so Alice had had to stay behind with her young son, hoping against hope that her husband would be able to work his own passage home someday, when his sentence ended. And now they were stuck, she slaving for her sister-in-law, and he bullied every day of his life, both of them living on the kindness—the doubtful kindness—of kin.

But not forever, he resolved very privately, following his mother up the lane. The hitch with Zach was the final straw, somehow—the last time he was going to act the poor relation for the amusement of his cousins. *I'll fix it, Mum. I swear. I'll run away to sea—or I'll go into the mines to work and earn passage for both of us.*

The only thing was, if he ran away to sea, he'd have to leave his mother behind, still trapped in his uncle's house. But boys his age didn't earn enough working in the tin mines, especially not these days, with good ore getting as scarce as shoals of pilchard.

Which left fishing on his uncle's boat, if he could bear it. Only, with four cousins ahead of him and three growing up behind, he couldn't see much future in *that,* either. Unbidden, a picture of Miss Emily Alexander rose in his mind's eye—the snotty, fair-haired girl in her clean, starched dress, living in that big house on the hill. . . . What did she know about earning a living? About being alone in the world, with no prospects and no savings to fall back on? Not much, if he was any judge, blind father or no blind father.

There had to be some job in Aldestow for a boy that didn't involve wrecking. One way or the other, one thing was sure: if there was, then Lewis Trelawny was going to find it.

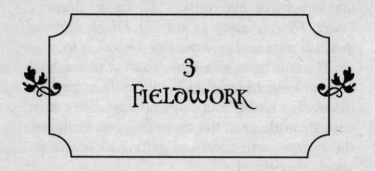

3
FIELDWORK

Emily ran from Aldestow Harbor as if demons were pursuing her. All she wanted was to get away. Away from Lewis Trelawny, away from Aldestow—away from Cornwall entirely.

Horrible boy, she thought feverishly. *Horrible rain, horrible harbor, horrible town. I hate this place!*

Running through the twisting, narrow streets, her vision blurry with the tears she would *not* shed, she ran full tilt into Mrs. Fidditch, the baker's wife.

"Why, Miss Emily!" A comfortably stout woman, Mrs. Fidditch always reminded Emily of a soft, plushy cat—and she was as curious as a cat, too, the biggest gossip in Aldestow, according to Mrs. Giffey. "Is something the matter?"

she asked avidly. Mrs. Fidditch knew good gossip when it ran straight into her. Emily flinched. First the boys on the dock, and now—it was too much. It was just *too much.*

"None of your business, you—you old cat," she said fiercely, swiping a sleeve across her tear-streaked face. "Find someone else to meow about for a change."

"Well, in all my born days!" Mrs. Fidditch gasped, bridling. "I dun't know as I ever—"

"Of course you don't," Emily snapped. "Why should you?"

Before Mrs. Fidditch could answer, Emily was off again, down the alleyway in back of the blacksmith's shop, knowing that she'd just done something supremely stupid, as bad as Thomas had ever done. *I've insulted the baker's wife. We'll have moldy scones and half-baked bread for weeks, unless Mrs. Giffey can make peace with her.*

But she still didn't stop. One more corner, at the little churchyard with its scattered gravestones, and she was out of the village entirely and up the hill toward Petherick Place. As soon as she found a break in the hedge, she cut across country, racing through bushes and brambles that caught at her skirt, until her heel caught on a clod of dirt and she fell headlong.

Wind knocked out of her, she clutched at the

ground, fingers digging into the soft earth. At least she was alone, with no one to see her rolling about on the hillside ... though doubtless Mrs. Fidditch would have a fine tale to tell in the village.

Turning over onto her back, she looked up at the sky. It was clearing, patches of brilliant blue becoming visible in the gray overcast. Now that her errand was done and she'd made a fool of herself, the weather improved. It would. *Mama, I miss you so. Why did you have to die and leave Papa and me all alone?*

As if Mama had wanted to die of a feverish cold—as if Papa didn't miss her, too ...

I try to take care of him, Mama, Emily thought, suddenly so exhausted that she wanted to cry. *I do try so hard. If it weren't for the accident, everything would be all right. ...*

But the accident had happened. James Alexander was blind, and Marian Petherick Alexander was dead, and nothing would ever be all right ever again. Squarely, Emily faced the unpleasant truth: there was no new commission from the Lighthouse Authority because no one wanted to hire a blind engineer, not even for the minor sort of consulting work that was all Papa could manage these days. Thomas was right, and so was that awful Trelawny boy—if it weren't for Mama's inheritance, she and Papa wouldn't have so much as a house to live in anymore . . . and there was nothing Emily could do about it, except keep on trying to do the impossible.

Nothing.

Wearily, she stood up and began to brush off her soiled clothing. It was time, and past time, to go home.

The front hall of Petherick Place was dark as she fumbled for her key, but there was light coming through the half-open door to her father's study. *He must be working with Thomas,* she thought. Pausing a moment at the foot of the stairs, she looked up at the magnificent portrait of her mother hanging opposite. Marian Petherick had been newly married when the painter had taken her likeness, and her happiness glowed in her dark blue eyes, so much brighter than her daughter's paler blue. Her chestnut hair, caught up in thick ringlets at the nape of her neck, glistened in the lamplight. Emily had always wished she had hair like that, instead of the fair, flyaway stuff that was always escaping from her combs.

"Hello, Mama," Emily said softly, as she always did when she was alone in the front hall.

Some people would have felt silly talking to a picture on the wall, but Emily never did. The portrait was all she had left of her mother; even her memories seemed less and less clear as the months went by. But she could always look at that painted face and remember. . . .

Voices, coming from her father's study—strangers' voices. A man and a woman, by the sound. Visitors? Not Cornish, from the accents—but they never had guests, and surely Papa would have told her that morning if he'd been expecting someone. Wouldn't he? The rooms would have had to be cleaned and aired, and fresh linens put on the beds—she'd have had to ask Mrs. Giffey to do something special for meals . . . and her clothes!

Oh, dear. Guiltily, she looked down at her snaggled and dirty skirts, trying futilely to tidy herself—but her hands were as muddy as her garments. *I can't let guests see me like this. I'd better slip upstairs for a wash and a change. . . .*

"Our only requirement is that the work be completed by the summer solstice," the man was saying. "Midsummer's Eve, you know."

"By June twenty-first, then," James Alexander said, sounding preoccupied. "Not much time . . . why the solstice?"

"Less than a month to work, counting from today," the man answered, as though he'd been asked how much time was available—which he hadn't been. Puzzled, Emily edged closer to the door. "I'm told that the tower itself is relatively sound, although extensive repairs will need to be

made to the interior. And of course, if you accept
the commission, you will have a completely free
hand."

A commission? She only just barely stopped
herself from clapping her hands with delight. *A
possible client! Oh, how wonderful!*

Hope surged in her heart, making her breath-
less. Perhaps that was why there had been
no package from the Lighthouse Authority—
perhaps the client had come in person to consult
with James Alexander! And—and—the man
must have seen by now that Papa was blind, and
he still wasn't making embarrassed, pitying
noises about how he was so sorry, he hadn't
known. . . .

Her father was talking again. Emily held her
breath to listen. "—admit that your proposal
intrigues me, sir. To rebuild a lighthouse of such
antiquity . . . well. Are you certain—that is, I
imagine you will wish to interview other lighthouse engineers before we agree to a contract."

"No other lighthouse engineer is available to
us, Mr. Alexander," said the woman. "Your background and experience suit our requirements
perfectly, if you don't mind my saying so."

"Of course not, I merely . . ." Now Papa
sounded flattered. "But surely—one of the
younger Stevenson brothers, perhaps . . ."

"No one," the woman told him, light and

laughing, but very firm. "Only you, if you will
consent to go."

Go? Go where? Oh, no! This wasn't just a con-
sultation. These people were talking as if—as if
Papa were still a working engineer, and they
wanted him to supervise the construction of a
lighthouse. But he couldn't do that kind of thing
anymore. Didn't they realize he couldn't? *He's
blind!*

"Papa, no!" Heedless of her looks, she pushed
through the study door. "You can't do fieldwork
again!"

Unfortunately, her preoccupation with her
father's voice had caused her to misjudge the
location of the others. Coming through the door,
she ran head-on into a tall young man dressed in
tweeds with an amused tilt to his mouth. She
would have fallen flat on the carpet if he hadn't
caught her by the shoulders and swung her
around.

"Hey there!" the visitor said, smiling down at
her as if more entertained than shocked at her
precipitous entrance. "Careful, young lady!"

Emily spared him one quick glance. "Papa, I
heard—"

"Emily." Her father sighed, and Thomas—
seated in the most comfortable chair—*tsk*ed dis-
approvingly. "Sir, madam, I apologize for my

daughter's behavior. Emily Elizabeth, these are our *guests*."

"I'm sorry, Papa," she said, blushing hotly, and for once very glad that he couldn't see her muddy skirts and generally bedraggled appearance. "I didn't mean to—to . . ."

She stopped, not quite sure what it was that she hadn't meant to do. But the young man who had caught her took no notice.

"No harm done," he said to her cheerfully. He smiled at the woman seated on the sofa, who was wearing a blue silk dress trimmed with lace. She had a pendant on a delicate gold chain around her neck, and she smiled back at the man—her husband?—with obvious affection. "Cassandra has been known to rush into a room or two in her time, so you see, I've practice."

"Why, so you have," the young woman— Cassandra—said in her merry, musical voice. She seemed to regard having had practice at catching rushing young ladies as a rare accomplishment. "It's a pleasure to meet you, my dear. No doubt you're interested in your father's work? I know I was always fascinated by *my* father's studies in mythology and legends—and now I find Edmund's biological researches intriguing as well."

"I—I don't think . . ." Emily wasn't quite sure

what to say to that, either. She was interested in her father's work, she supposed, but only because it *was* Papa's work. Fortunately, her father saved her from having to finish the sentence.

"That's another point to be considered," he said, frowning. It made the scars on his cheeks curl grotesquely, dragging one side of his mouth down—but Emily didn't think he knew that. "If I do accept this commission—and I haven't agreed that I will yet—what's to be done with Emily? An engineering site is no place for a child."

It was no place for a blind man, either, but no one in the room seemed willing to mention *that*. Emily opened her mouth to say so and was forestalled.

"Take her with you," Cassandra said promptly, one hand playing with the pendant at her throat. "Captain Malachi and his crew will take very good care of her."

"Besides, I suspect you'll discover that this is no ordinary engineering site, sir," her husband interjected. He and his wife exchanged glances, and Emily got the feeling there was a great deal being left unsaid. The idea made her nervous. "Given the location, that is."

"Hmm. Well, if you're certain, I suppose we could give it a try. . . ." James Alexander sounded dubious—but somehow, Emily knew that he was talking about far more than the matter of whether or not she should come with him.

"I am quite certain," Cassandra said firmly, folding her hands in her lap. It was probably a trick of the light, but the pendant of her necklace appeared to be glowing. Emily tried not to stare. What sort of a stone *was* that? It was almost the color of a golden topaz, but no topaz would shine so brightly. "You are a man of vision, Mr. Alexander. I'm sure that young Emily will be very useful to you in your labors—as will one other, I believe."

She means Thomas, of course, Emily thought, biting back a sharp comment. The secretary was preening smugly from his place next to the fire.

"The fee is certainly very tempting," he said, as if Cassandra had spoken to him. Trust him to mention money! "Quite generous. Even considering that we must make such a long ocean voyage to the site."

"Oh, I doubt that anyone would find a voyage aboard the *Basset* to be *too* tedious, sir," Cassandra told him, sounding amused for some reason Emily didn't bother to wonder at. "She's a most comfortable and commodious vessel."

Emily started. The *Basset*! That was the strange little ship she'd watched sail so skillfully past the sands at the harbor mouth—an ocean-going vessel. What *were* these people up to? This

Edmund and Cassandra—they couldn't possibly be serious! Maybe the commission was an impossible one, and they'd been turned down by every other engineer they'd approached. "Papa, if you try to do fieldwork again—"

"I know, my dear," he said, but he wasn't really listening. There was a note in his voice that she hadn't heard in ages—genuine interest and excitement. *He didn't even ask what the Lighthouse Authority had sent him,* she realized, eyes stinging. *And I was so worried—it's as if he's got something more important to think about now. Real work to do, at last. Oh, Papa . . .*

Torn by conflicting emotions, she slipped out of the study and back into the hall to lean against the wall under the portrait of her mother. *Mama, what can I do? I can't stop him. I'm not even sure I should.*

The rustle of silk skirts alerted her barely in time to stand up straight.

"Is that your mother?" Cassandra said, looking up at the portrait. "She's lovely."

Emily looked away, making her voice go cold and flat. "She's dead."

"I know." Cassandra looked grave. "So is my mother."

"Do you—do you miss her?" She winced at the personal question coming out of her own mouth—as bad as anything Mrs. Fidditch had ever asked—but Cassandra didn't seem to mind.

"All the time," she said simply. "Your father *will* be all right, Emily. You'll see. He's a very fine engineer."

"He's blind!" Emily said passionately. *I know my father is a fine engineer! Or he was . . . but what difference does* that *make?* "You know he's blind. I promised Mama I'd take care of him, but she didn't—you don't—he can't *see*! If he tries to supervise an engineering site again—"

Appalled, she clapped both hands over her mouth. What had come over her, talking like that to a stranger? *If she tells Papa what I said, he'll never forgive me.*

And yet, a part of her wished that Cassandra would do just that. If anything could bring Papa to his senses . . .

"Oh. I see." Cassandra nodded gravely. "You don't believe he can do it."

Emily's mouth fell open. She closed it with an angry snap.

"Of course I do," she said rigidly. "But *you* don't, not really. You can't, if you know anything about engineering. He'll have to draw up the designs, organize the quarry for dressing the stone and the frame, and supervise the workmen. And a blind man—I don't know what you're playing at, but you can't possibly want to hire him for this sort of commission. No one would."

"But we do," Cassandra said very seriously. Her expression was sympathetic but certain. "The *Basset* sailed for him, you see, and the motto of the *Basset* is *Credendo vides*. Or, to put it another way, 'By believing, one sees.' He needs you, my dear."

Emily blinked. Of course her father needed her. But what did that have to do with the strange words on the little ship's banner? And—the ship had sailed for him? She didn't understand. "What do you mean?"

"I mean that seeing is less important than believing," Cassandra said, smiling brilliantly. "Your father needs to believe in himself, Emily—and so do you. Sailing on the *Basset* will be good for both of you. Wait and see."

With that, she turned and walked calmly back into the study, leaving a very confused Emily staring after her. "By believing, one sees"? Papa couldn't see. That was the whole problem. Wasn't it?

Seeing and believing . . . it was insane. As insane as hiring a blind engineer to build a lighthouse. And yet Cassandra *seemed* perfectly rational.

Wait and see. . . .

She could hear her father's voice again through the half-open door, eagerly discussing tools and reference works and possible construction schedules with Thomas and Edmund. Maybe—maybe he could do this, with help. And if it made him feel useful—feel *able*—again, despite all the things he couldn't do for himself . . . well. Ship's motto or none, perhaps the voyage would be worth the risk.

And they would be leaving Cornwall, too, so the weather might even be better.

One last time, she glanced up at the portrait. *I will take care of him, Mama. I'll keep my promise somehow. I swear.*

4
THIEF-TAKEN

After thinking long and hard for several days, Lewis had managed to come up with only one possible way to earn money in Aldestow, and not much, at that: he could get some sort of job on the wharf. But to do that, he had to ask his uncle for help.

At first, Uncle Josiah didn't seem inclined to oblige.

"A job?" he said, setting aside the bit of sail he'd been mending. No man in Aldestow considered sewing to be women's work; there was too much of it to be done on a ship. "What sort of a job?"

"Any sort, Uncle," Lewis said, swallowing. "Well—any sort but goin' out for salvage. Mum won't—"

He stopped, not wanting to complain about

his mother, but Uncle Jos only nodded. "Aye, Alice is stubborn that way. I dun't know as I can blame her—but I haven't a place for you on the *Maid,* boy, not with the fishin' as bad as it's been. Could be next year . . ."

Next year he'd be thirteen. He couldn't wait that long. "I know ye dun't, Uncle. There's Martin an' Denny—an' next year, Timothy will be old enough to go out in good weather, too. That's why I thought—well, if you could speak to someone on the wharf, some friend of yours, I could do *something* to earn my keep. An' Mum's. Errands an' such."

"Earn yer keep?" His uncle gave him a sharp glance. "Are you not satisfied with conditions living in my house?"

"No, no! I mean—it isn't that." He stopped, groping for words that would be true and yet not disrespectful. "I'm grateful to you and Aunt Kate." Well, that was almost true. "But I'm the man o' the family now. 'Tis my responsibility, until Dad comes home. . . ."

He'd struck the right note, he saw with relief; Uncle Jos was mollified.

"That's so, you are. I hadn't thought of it that way." He paused, turning the thought over in his mind. "Hmm. Well, could be I could ask Jacob Sweeney to take you on. He's been talkin' about a boy to run errands an' sweep up. Old

Caleb Colcannon is getting a bit past it. . . ."

"Mr. Sweeney, the receiving agent? That would be perfect," Lewis said eagerly. "Thank you, Uncle!"

His uncle held up a warning hand. "'Tis only a chance, mind. And if Jacob does take you on, I'll expect you to give him a fair day's work. No slackin' off, nor any more hitchin' with that Zach o' mine. If you mean to take a man's part, then you must *act* the man and not the boy. Understand?"

"Aye, Uncle," he said more soberly. He couldn't blame Uncle Jos for being cautious, not after offering to speak up for his unregarded nephew. It was better than he'd hoped for, really—all he asked was a chance. "I understand. I'll make you proud, I swear I will."

"Humph." Josiah Trelawny turned back to his neat stitching. "Well, we'll see what Jacob says."

But Josiah Trelawny and Jacob Sweeney had been boys together, and—after a certain amount of hemming and hawing, and haggling over salary—Sweeney took Lewis on, right enough. Though he wasn't entirely enthusiastic about his new employee.

"No messin' about on my wharf," he warned, swiveling his chair so that he could look Lewis straight in the eyes. "No watchin' ships as they come into harbor or go out, no markin' cargo so

the wreckers will know which grounded ships
are worth turnin' out for—you do your job and
keep your nose clean, and, well, we'll see how it
goes. Understand?"

Just like Uncle Josiah, Lewis thought, keeping
his face expressionless with an effort. But Uncle
Jos at least hadn't alluded to his father's reputa-
tion for wrecking as something that might be
held against Lewis. As if every man, woman, and
child in Aldestow didn't follow the harbor's com-
ings and goings, just in case! *Does he think I'm a
fool? Of course I understand.*

Aloud, he said only: "Yes, sir. Where do I
start?"

"Outside, with a sweep-up," Sweeney said,
nodding toward a battered broom leaning in a
corner of the receiving office. "Last cargo loaded
yesterday evening was cattle, an' they left a mess
all over the dock. When you finish that—not too
long, mind!—come back and I'll tell you what to
do next. If there's anything."

Sweeping up stale cow chips on a warm
spring day was not Lewis's idea of a pleasant
task, even when he could sweep them straight
into the water of the harbor, but he didn't argue.
"Yes, sir," he said again, grabbing the broom. *I'll
show you,* he thought. *I'll show everyone.*

He hadn't mentioned the new job to his
mother yet. He had a feeling that Alice Trelawny

wouldn't exactly approve. She seemed to think that *she* should be the one taking care of *him*. As though he were still the baby boy Zach had accused him of being. Best to tell her later, after he'd been working for a while. . . .

Outside, the wharf was busy enough. Following his nose, Lewis found the place where the cattle had made a mess and commenced sweeping with a great deal of energy. He was very aware that Mr. Sweeney was watching him through the dusty panes of the receiving office's little window. So the agent was checking on him, was he? Let him check.

I'm doing it, Dad, he thought almost gleefully. The cow chips flew. *I'm earning my—our— passage to Australia.*

For a while, he was so intent on his task that he didn't pay much attention to his surroundings—certainly, he never glanced toward the harbor, or the ships waiting at mooring to be loaded or unloaded. He didn't want Sweeney to accuse him of marking cargo! Then a particularly vigorous sweep of the old broom resulted in a startled "Oh!" and he looked up to find that the ragged bristles had snagged on the dainty blue silk skirts of a woman.

"I'm sorry," he gasped, horrified beyond belief. This wasn't just any woman from the village, either. This was the new foreigner, the

Englishwoman who had come to stay at Petherick Place with the Alexanders. Everyone in town
had wondered why she and her husband were
visiting—and now he'd gone and swept cow drop-
pings on her skirts! *And* her elegant, high-button
leather shoes, he noticed, writhing inwardly. "I
didn't mean—I didn't see—" Frantically, he tried
to pull the bristles free of the delicate cloth but
only succeeded in tangling them worse. "I'm
sorry. . . ."

"Goodness, you have got things in a muddle,"
she said, laughing. She was slender and fair, he
saw, with lovely eyes—the same blue as his
mum's—and a generous smile. He winced inter-
nally, wishing miserably that he'd never been
born. "Don't worry. Here, let me do that."

Stooping gracefully, she twisted the filthy
bristles with her fingers, apparently not the least
bit disturbed by the smell. When she straightened, her skirts were free and her hands were
smeared with dirt.

"There, that's better," she said, with every
evidence of satisfaction. Pulling a dainty square
of lace out of her pocket, she proceeded to wipe
her hands clean with it, and then, touching the
handkerchief only with her fingertips, she
dropped it over the railing into the water. "No
harm done."

Lewis stared at her dumbly. Her obviously

very expensive skirts were snagged beyond
repair—he knew, he'd watched his mum try
to repair damage like that on less delicate
material—and she'd thrown away her fancy lace
handkerchief . . . and now she said that no harm
had been done?

"I—I *am* sorry," he said again, as if repeated
apologies would make a difference. *Uncle Jos
always says that the gentry are different from nor-
mal folks. Maybe he's right.* "I didn't see you."

"Of course you didn't," she said, smiling and
holding out one cleaned hand. Without thinking,
he took it, and found his own hand being heartily
shaken. "My name is Cassandra. What's yours?"

For all the world as if they were the same age
and had just been introduced to each other at
high tea. Lewis choked. She was different, all
right. He'd never had *any* grown woman speak to
him that way—nor any grown man, either.

"Um—I'm Lewis," he managed finally. "Lewis
Trelawny. I live in Aldestow."

"I suspected you did," she said confidingly.
With one hand, she toyed with something at
her throat—a necklace of some sort, but he
didn't dare look too closely. She might think he
wanted to steal it or something. Who could tell?
Her eyes had narrowed slightly, as if she were
musing over something very serious and a little
surprising. "Tell me, Lewis, have you ever

thought of taking a sea voyage? To explore strange new lands and learn new things . . ."

"You mean run away to sea?" Nonplussed, he stared at her. How could she have guessed that he'd been considering doing just that only a few days before? She couldn't, of course. It was just a coincidence, but he was nervously aware that his face had reddened guiltily at her question. "I— no! Why would I do a thing like that?"

"Not run away to sea," she said, as if it were the most natural and logical thing in the world— as if she weren't talking absolute nonsense. "Take a voyage—on *that* ship." She pointed one elegant finger at a little ship floating quietly in the harbor—the same little ship that had sailed so dangerously through the harbor mouth at low tide on the day Emily Alexander had blacked his eye. "The *Basset*. She's very good at sailing to distant lands."

She must be, Lewis thought, bemused. *She certainly wouldn't be much good for anything else!* Seen close to, the *Basset* was an even stranger vessel than he'd realized at first: all useless swirls and ornamental carving, more like a rich man's toy than an honest sailing ship. And now that he came to look at them, wasn't her crew, well, rather short? *Shorter than I am, every one.*

"I dun't want to leave Aldestow," he told the woman, trying not be rude. *And if I did, it wouldn't be on that silly-looking ship! Give me a decent fishing boat any day of the week.* "I can't leave my mum."

"Ah." She nodded as though she understood. Perhaps she did, but he doubted it. "I suppose you feel that you have to be sensible. My sister Miranda would certainly understand that! But sailing on the *Basset,* you'd be back almost before anyone knew you were gone. And Mr. Alexander and Emily would appreciate the company of someone else from Aldestow on their voyage. . . ."

Mr. Alexander and Emily . . . Were the blind man and his daughter going to be sailing on this HMS *Basset*? It seemed so. They were standing at the gangplank with that secretary fellow, the one who looked like an overstuffed pillow. With them was a lean young man who was probably Cassandra's husband. But gentry or not, this Cassandra definitely had windmills in her head if she thought that either of the Alexanders would be pleased by the companionship of an Aldestow wrecker's boy—especially Emily!

"Much you know about it," he said, the words out before he considered what they might sound like—and then stopped, appalled. If that wasn't being rude, then he didn't know what was! "I mean—"

"I know what you meant," she said serenely.

"Nonetheless, I believe—when you've had time to consider the matter—that you'll find I'm right. *Credendo vides,* you know. 'By believing, one sees.' If I speak to Captain Malachi, I'm sure he'd be glad to welcome you aboard."

"What?" *Captain who?*

"Think about it," she advised, smiling at him.

With that, she moved off to join the little group by the gangplank. Lewis stared after her in astonishment. She *did* go up to one of the odd little men who seemed to make up the *Basset*'s crew—a sturdy fellow with a red beard and a pipe, who shook his head when Cassandra gestured toward Lewis. Then he shrugged, as if agreeing. The ship's captain? And if so, was he touched in the head, too?

Standing next to her father on the other side of the gangplank, Emily turned just in time to catch him staring after Cassandra—well, at them all, he supposed. The girl made a face, a really nasty one, and then very deliberately turned her back to him.

Well, of all the cheek! So he'd been looking. So what? He'd as much right to look as anyone. *I hope she sails straight off the edge of the world, I do!* Aldestow would be a better place without her—*and* her father, poor blind man though he was.

Some instinct made him glance behind him,

and he realized that Sweeney was watching him
through the window again—watching and shaking his head in disapproval. It figured. Just at the
moment he paused.

Well, it could have been worse. Sweeney
could have decided to check on him just in time
to see Lewis scatter cow manure all over that
Cassandra's skirts. She might be a lunatic, but
she was definitely gentry.

Furiously, he applied himself to his sweeping
again. He'd just found a way to earn some money
to support himself and his mother, and he was
not about to lose his opportunity just because
some foreigner thought he ought to go on a sea
voyage, of all things! Not run away to sea, either,
but go *sailing*—as if he were a rich man's son. . . .

*Wonder if that's what snotty Miss Alexander
and her father are doing?* he thought, resisting
the impulse to look at them again. Sometimes
sick rich people went on sea voyages to get well
again, he'd heard, and Mr. Alexander had certainly been ill enough for that. Not that Lewis
cared.

A tiny metallic clink caught his attention,
something swept up by the broom. Curious, he
bent to inspect the bristles and came up with a
sort of a jewel or stone on a bit of chain. Now
where had that come from? He turned the little
thing in his hand so that it sparkled bright

yellow-gold in the sunlight. *Pretty. Mum could maybe make a button out of it or something. . . .*

"My necklace!" Over by the *Basset*'s gangplank, Cassandra cried out, her hands going to her throat in alarm. "It's gone!"

She'd been fooling with something around her neck when she'd been talking to him. The little jewel could well have been a pendant. Likely, she'd broken the chain and it had fallen.

"Here it is," he said impulsively, holding out his hand. "Is this it?"

"Cassandra, he's got your necklace," Emily said, outraged. "Right there in his hand!"

Lewis looked down, confused. Well, of course it would be in his hand, once he'd picked it up. Where else? "I just found it—" *On the dock,* he started to say, but he didn't have a chance to finish.

"Stolen, no doubt," the fussy English secretary man said. "You're the Trelawny boy, aren't you. Hum. Blood will tell, I suppose. Sweeney! Get out here!"

"I didn't steal anything," Lewis said furiously, but he could feel himself going white. Thief-taken, he could be in serious trouble. Transported, even, like his dad, and what would Mum do then? "I found it on the dock. The chain's broken."

At the same time, Emily spoke up. "Don't be

silly, Thomas. I didn't mean to say—Cassandra! Tell Thomas that Lewis didn't steal your necklace."

"Oh, there it is," Cassandra said, the alarm immediately fading from her expression. Walking across the wharf, she held out one hand to Lewis. Relieved, he dropped the pendant into it. There. That was that. "Thank you. Of course Lewis didn't steal anything. Who ever said that he did?"

"What's this, what's this?" Sweeney bustled self-importantly out of his office. "What's the boy done?"

"I've done nothing!" Lewis cried. *I should have swept the silly thing into the harbor!* Why wouldn't anyone listen to him? Or to Cassandra and Emily?

"Stolen this lady's necklace," Thomas said, nodding at Cassandra as if she hadn't just told him the opposite. "A valuable piece of jewelry. Diamond, wasn't it?"

"Not diamond," Cassandra said, sounding irritated. Maybe she didn't like Thomas any more than Lewis did. She turned her palm outward, the pendant glittering goldenly against it. "*Really,* Mr. Bentham. It's nothing like a diamond."

Sweeney wasn't interested in accuracy, either. "A diamond necklace! I might have known," he

said with relish. "Like father, like son. Poor Jos
Trelawny. He always set such store by his family.
Not to worry, ma'am. We don't tolerate thieves
here in Aldestow."

"I'm not a thief!" Agonized, Lewis looked
around the dock for help—for anyone. He'd have
welcomed even Zachary at this point. "My dad
wasn't a thief!"

Panicked, he shoved the secretary fellow
with both hands, forgetting that he still held the
broom in one of them. A surprised Bentham staggered backward, the broomstick taking him in
the knees—or did Cassandra's extended foot
catch his heel? No, it couldn't have been. But the
next thing Lewis knew, there was a magnificent
splash from the harbor.

"Help! Help!" Three feet from the ladder,
Thomas flailed around like a human waterwheel.
"I can't swim!"

"Man overboard!" Cassandra called, her clear
voice echoing the length of the wharf.

She was laughing! Why was she laughing?
There was nothing funny in a man drowning,
even a man like Thomas Bentham. Lewis made
an abortive move to help, but he wasn't needed.
Men were already rushing from every corner of
the dock. One lay full-length on the boards and
extended a fishing gaff to the sputtering man.
Thomas didn't seem to see it. His waistcoat had

come undone and was floating up around his armpits.

"Help! He—*gluggle*—he-elp!"

"Oh, my goodness!" Emily clapped both hands over her mouth, looking guilty. "Oh, poor Thomas. I'm sorry, but *doesn't* he look silly."

"Very silly," Cassandra agreed with a chuckle, fastening the chain of her pendant again. "Quickly now. There's no time to waste."

She took Lewis by one arm and Emily by the other and began to urge them both along the wharf.

"I'm not a thief," Lewis tried to tell her, lagging behind—or trying to. Cassandra was having none of it.

"I know, I know, but that's neither here nor there," she said briskly.

"What about Thomas?" Emily asked, sounding as bewildered as Lewis felt. "He won't drown, will he?"

"With all of these good people around?" Cassandra's eyebrows lifted. "I should very much doubt it."

She didn't sound as though she cared very much, either. In the water, Thomas's cries had risen to a high pitch, like the wails of a baby; one of the would-be rescuers had apparently crowned him with a life preserver.

"Ow! Ow! Ow!"

"Throw him a rope!" Sweeney shouted, leaning ineffectually over the water. "Don't worry, sir, we'll save you!"

Lewis had his doubts. Before he could voice them, he and Emily were being hurried up the *Basset*'s gangplank, and then, all at once, they were on the ship itself, looking back at Cassandra and her husband standing on the wharf.

"Bon voyage!" they shouted, both waving enthusiastically. "Fair sailing!"

Lewis was staring at the shore—at the rapidly *receding* shore. With both hands, he gripped the ship's rail as water widened between him and Aldestow wharf—between him and everyone and everything he'd ever known.

"No," he said very softly—then shouted, "No! I don't want to go with you! Take me back! Please take me back! I can't—"

Too late. The *Basset* was already under full sail, making for the harbor mouth. It was just on high tide, so she'd glide through like a swan— and if her captain came about, he'd miss the tide.

Without intending to in the least, Lewis Trelawny had run away to sea.

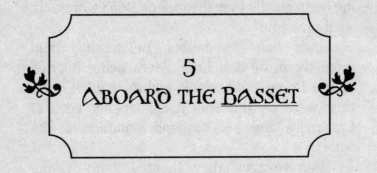

5
ABOARD THE BASSET

Aboard the *Basset,* everything seemed to be happening at once. Emily stood next to her father, holding on to his arm to steady him—and herself—as she watched the chaos swirling around them. The remarkable crew she had scarcely had time to meet rushed about like mad things, winding the anchor and hoisting sails, and swarming and scampering through the rigging like so many monkeys.

"Trim the mainsail!" Captain Malachi roared, his red fringe of a beard quivering with energy. "Bosun Eli, you have the watch. Eyes ahead for squalls. Helmsman Archimedes, set our course!"

"Aye, aye, Captain!"

"Aye, sir!"

They *were* a remarkable crew, even to look at.

Not a one was over three feet tall. They looked like dwarves, but surely that was nonsense. Wasn't it? At that, the dwarves weren't as bad as the others—the very little crew members wearing red jackets, top hats, and *spats*.

They're so <u>*small*</u>, she thought nervously, trying not to stare. As if he felt her looking at him, one of the little men paused in front of her, head tilted sideways. Then he removed his hat and *bowed* before scampering off. Startled, Emily moved just a bit closer to her father. *What was* <u>*that*</u> *all about?*

"Emily?" James Alexander sounded alarmed; he was very sensitive, and she didn't usually cling *quite* so closely. "Emmie, what's the matter? Where's Thomas?"

Oh, dear, he doesn't realize Thomas has been left behind, she thought, heart sinking. *And he isn't going to be happy to hear about it, either. . . .*

"Thomas isn't here, Papa," she told him bravely. "He fell in the water and got left behind. We've brought that Lewis Trelawny boy from the village instead."

Put that way, it sounded ridiculous—as though Lewis were a replacement for Thomas. Her father clearly didn't believe a word of it.

"What?" he exclaimed, his voice rising. "The Trelawny boy—but my secretary! I need him to take notes for me. We must go back at once!"

"I don't think we can, Papa," she said, shading her eyes to see the rapidly disappearing shoreline. "We're already out of the harbor. If we go back now, we'll miss the tide."

"But—"

At that moment, Lewis, who had been standing stock-still, as if in shock, made a desperate lunge for the ship's rail. For an awful second, Emily thought he was going to try to swim all the way back to Aldestow, but then he clapped one hand over his mouth and bent double so that the top half of him almost disappeared over the railing. Retching frantically, he seemed to be puking up the entire contents of his body clear down to his shoes. Two of the odd little crew members grabbed him, one by each ankle, and hung on, grinning gleefully all over their funny round faces.

"Oh, dear, oh, dear." An older dwarf with a long, flowing white beard rushed over to inspect Lewis. "My, my, my."

"*Now* what's happening?" James asked sharply. He hated to hear sounds that he couldn't identify, and Emily doubted very much if he'd ever heard anything like the awful gasping and sobbing noises that Lewis was making.

"Nothing serious, Papa," Emily sniffed, pulling back just a little from the heaving boy. *She* didn't feel the least bit unwell, and a good thing, too. "Lewis—the Trelawny boy is being seasick, that's all."

I suppose he can't help it, she thought, trying to be charitable and failing miserably. *Although—how odd. Isn't his uncle a fisherman? Surely he must have been on a boat before. . . .*

The retching noises mercifully ceased, and Lewis went limp, collapsing into a damp, smelly puddle.

"Ohhh," he groaned, a long, dying fall. "I'm not seasick. I can't be seasick. I dun't *get* seasick!"

Well, he certainly was now. Critically, Emily inspected him. His broad, ordinary-looking features had gone dead white under the sallow complexion, and his teeth chattered.

"There, there, you just rest for a little and let old Sebastian take care of you," the elderly dwarf fussed kindly, helping him to lean back against the rail. "You'll feel better soon, I've no doubt."

Suddenly, the ship lifted and lurched. Lewis curled up into a ball, moaning and clutching at his middle.

"*Tsk.* Poor lad." Stepping back, the dwarf Sebastian turned to Captain Malachi and saluted. "Regret to inform you, sir, that our latest passenger is indisposed," he said solemnly.

Emily stifled a giggle. *Indisposed!* She should think *so*. If Lewis had been any more indisposed, he'd have gone right overboard.

"Seasick, is he?" the captain said, not sounding particularly surprised or dismayed. Well, she supposed sick landlubbers wouldn't be all that strange an experience for an oceangoing ship's captain. "Poor lad. First Mate Sebastian, we're shorthanded just now, as you know, so get him below and settled quickly."

"Aye, aye, sir." Sebastian saluted again. "Come on, then, there's a brave lad. . . ."

"Captain, this is intolerable!" James Alexander stormed, turning his head toward the sound of Malachi's voice. The scars framing his blind eyes flamed red, throbbing with emotion. They only did so when he was seriously upset, Emily knew. "I must protest. We've literally kidnapped the boy—and I want my secretary!"

It was clear to Emily whose plight mattered more; Lewis obviously came in a poor second in her father's mind.

"Now, now, no need to get in such an uproar, Mr. Engineer Alexander," Captain Malachi said soothingly. "Miss Cassandra said that the *Basset* sailed for you, sir, not for your secretary. *You* are the man we want—and your daughter and the boy, too, it seems."

"But my *secretary*—he had half of my books in his trunks—"

"We will not turn back, Mr. Engineer," the

captain said inflexibly. "We've a fine library on board ship, with all the books you'll ever want, and Helmsman Archimedes can help you read them. It's your knowledge that's needed, not your secretary. We will contrive."

"My knowledge! The work would be difficult enough *with* Thomas—" He stopped, intemperate words obviously hovering on his lips. Emily could feel his arm trembling under her hand. Taking a deep breath, he started to speak more slowly but no less intensely. "And the boy—if he comes with us to the work site, I'll be responsible for his safety as well as for Emily's!"

Emily didn't like that idea one bit.

"*You* aren't responsible for Lewis, Papa," she said, seriously alarmed. *If Papa believes he has to take care of Lewis—and me . . . I never thought of that!* "It wasn't your fault he came aboard. And I can take care of myself."

"Emmie." Her father turned his face down to her, blind eyes searching—almost as if he'd forgotten she was there holding on to his arm. "You are a child, my daughter. The boy—Lewis?—is a child. I am an adult, the only one on board the boy knows from home. That means I am responsible for both of you."

His words took on a leaden quality, as if he were reading one of the syllogisms he'd used to explain formal logic to her. *If A equals B, and B equals C, then A must also equal C. . . .*

"Right you are, Mr. Engineer," Captain Malachi said cheerfully, much to Emily's dismay. Couldn't he see that her father was the one who needed taking care of, not the other way around? "Of course, Sebastian is capable of dealing with an upset stomach or two—but as you say, you're from the boy's own home. It's a good thing you're with us, all around."

If Captain Malachi's reaction wasn't what she'd expected, her father's was even worse. James Alexander took a deep breath, squaring his shoulders. "Yes. When you put it that way . . . I suppose it is."

No! He couldn't believe that—it was worse than the day when she'd come home to find her father in the study planning to try fieldwork again. And again, there wasn't anything she could do about it. *We have to go home again— back for Thomas. If we don't . . .*

Captain Malachi didn't agree with her. The *Basset* sailed on.

In the ensuing days, her father spent much of his time in his cabin or closeted in the ship's library with Helmsman Archimedes. The *Basset* did have a great many books on engineering; they even had Alan Stevenson's new *Report on the Construction of the Skerryvore Light.* That helped.

So did Archimedes. The *Basset*'s helmsman was a sturdy dwarf with a black-and-silver beard and a grave bearing. He was a sailor, not an engineer, but he seemed to know as much as Thomas on the subject, anyway. Emily knew that her father was much impressed by his quick wits. With his daughter to take notes for him and Archimedes to create diagrams from his descriptions, James Alexander was soon well on the way to forgetting his secretary entirely.

For herself, Emily found Helmsman Archimedes as disturbing as he was comforting.

"Don't you fret, Miss Emily," Archimedes reassured her on the third day out of Aldestow. They were standing in the corridor outside the library, talking in low voices. "Your father and I, we understand each other. Between us, we'll get this lighthouse built. I have faith in him."

"Oh, so do I," she said quickly, feeling vaguely ashamed. Because, she realized sickly, the truth was that she didn't—not like Archimedes and Captain Malachi. They were both so sure that James Alexander could do whatever needed to be done, and Emily wasn't. Not really. *Cassandra said that I didn't believe—but he simply <u>can't</u> do everything that he could before. Can he?* "Only . . ."

It was so strange. Here she was, sailing off to who-knew-where on a mysterious ship crewed by dwarves and gremlins—Archimedes had told her that the very little crew members were gremlins ("When they aren't working mischief, that is; then we call them other things!")—and she still couldn't make herself believe the impossible.

"Emily!" Her father's voice, from the library; he'd been shouting a great deal lately, much as he always used to when supervising an engineering site, and a closed door did nothing to muffle him. "Emily Elizabeth, where are you? Where's Archimedes? I need the numbers for the focal plane calculations again!"

"Coming, Papa," she called, grimacing apologetically at the dignified dwarf.

Archimedes only winked at her, completely undisturbed by her father's peremptory tone. "I have the figures all ready, Engineer," he said cheerfully, opening the library door. "Just as you requested."

James Alexander ran one hand through his hair distractedly. "Good. I've had an idea."

And they were off again.

Lewis continued to be ill, rarely leaving the small cabin toward the stern of the ship that had been turned into a sickroom for him. First Mate Sebastian was worried about him and said so; Emily wasn't, much. He was only seasick, after all. People didn't die of being seasick.

She didn't like to think about the Aldestow

boy. If he hadn't picked up Cassandra's pendant, the whole problem with Thomas might never have happened. Uneasily, she was aware that she was being, well, maybe a little unfair—Lewis certainly hadn't deserved to be accused of stealing, and Cassandra had almost shoved him on board the *Basset* there at the end—but Emily couldn't help what she felt.

Serves him right if he's sick, she thought defiantly. *And if Cassandra wanted him to come with us for some reason—well, let her worry about him! I've got more important things to do.*

Then, on the afternoon of the sixth day out of Aldestow, she was on deck taking some wave measurements for her father—using the ship's *wuntarlabe,* the amazing copper-and-silver device that steered the *Basset*—when four gremlins hurried past, laden down with cushions and lap robes. When she turned around to see what they were up to, Lewis was there, being settled into a deck chair by a solicitous Sebastian.

Emily hadn't even known that the *Basset* carried deck chairs.

"There you go, lad," the kindly old dwarf said, fussing about his patient with the lap robe and the cushions. "A bit of sun will do you good—put some color in those pale cheeks of yours."

Lewis grunted, leaning back in the chair with his eyes closed.

He does look dreadful, Emily thought critically, considering him. *Fish-belly white and sort of greenish at the same time. I think he's lost weight, too.* Which wasn't a surprise, now that she came to think of it. *Maybe you really can die of seasickness. . . .*

She hoped not. So far, James Alexander had seemed willing to let Sebastian take care of the Aldestow boy, at least until they got wherever it was they were going. If Lewis got sicker, Emily didn't like to think what her father would do.

"What're *you* lookin' at?" Lewis asked without opening his eyes.

She jumped slightly. "How did you know I— what do you mean?"

"Felt you starin'." He opened his eyes then, but only to glare up at her balefully. "Think it's funny, do you? Me bein' sick."

"I don't think about it at all, usually," she said, not quite honestly. "Or about you."

"Well, good," he muttered. "I dun't, either. Think about you, I mean. What's that thing yer usin'?"

"This?" She glanced down at the central wheel of the *wuntarlabe,* glittering in the warmth of the sun. "It's called a *wuntarlabe.* Normally, it steers the ship, but I'm using it to take wave measurements."

"How does it work?" he asked curiously.

She shrugged. "I don't know. Helmsman
Archimedes set it for me, and I just write down
the numbers. Papa says it's like an astrolabe—
that's a device for calculating the height of astro-
nomical objects, like the sun or the stars—only
different."

"Steers the ship, does it? Dun't look like it's
attached to any rudder," he said, craning his
neck. "What did you call it? A wonder-lubber?"

"Wuntarlabe," she said primly. "I think. And I
told you, I don't know how it works."

"Oh. Too bad," he said, settling back into his
chair with a sigh. As if her answer didn't really
matter—though he *had* asked. "Might have been
interesting."

He's sick, she reminded herself. *He needs to
save his strength.*

For a while, Emily worked in silence broken
only by the flapping of the *Basset*'s blue-and-gold
banner and the wooden creaking noises of a ship
under full sail. Even the waves were relatively
calm—perhaps that was why First Mate Sebastian had suggested that Lewis come on deck. If
so, it wasn't working. The Aldestow boy was now
as green as grass.

Eventually, Lewis spoke again.

"I'm not a thief, you know," he said.

"What?" Confused by the shift in subject,
Emily frowned.

"I said I'm not a thief." He was staring at the *wuntarlabe* again, but not as if he were really seeing it. "Whatever that puffy-faced Englishman thought—I didn't steal the lady's necklace."

"I know," she said, flushing slightly. "I never said you did. That was all Thomas."

"You pointed me out to him," he said. Clearly, the memory rankled.

"Yes, well . . . I didn't mean it. No, really," she insisted. "I did tell him he was wrong, remember? He just wouldn't listen. Besides, Cassandra said—" *Oops.* She hadn't really meant to mention Cassandra.

"What did Cassandra say?" he asked, eyes narrowing suspiciously. "Somethin' about me?"

"Not exactly. It's just . . ." Emily hesitated. Cassandra had said a lot of things that she didn't particularly want to talk about to Lewis—or to anyone else. "She told my father that the people who sailed with him would help him build the lighthouse. I thought she meant Thomas and me, but when all the fuss happened and she pushed you on board, she—I think she intended for you to sail with us all along. Or from the moment she saw you on the wharf, at least."

"What?" Startled, he reared up in his chair, jaw hanging. "I know she pushed me, but I didn't—you mean *that's* why I'm here? Because some silly woman took one look at me an' decided I was just the person to go an' build a lighthouse?"

"Papa's going to do the building," Emily corrected him. This was embarrassing, but why else would Cassandra have shoved Lewis up the gangplank like that? And Captain Malachi, too— thinking back, Emily realized that he'd also been willing to accept Lewis on board the *Basset* right from the first. "We're just supposed to help. Somehow."

"Well, that's just marvelous, isn't it," Lewis said, richly disgusted. He didn't seem inclined to give her an argument, she noticed. But then, he was the one who had been pushed. "A fat lot of good I'm going to be to anyone if I'm always pukin' my guts in a bucket!"

"Papa hasn't asked you for help yet," she said, nettled. "He has Archimedes and me. Maybe he won't need you. Anyway, you won't be seasick forever. Sooner or later, we'll reach this island we're going to, and then you'll be on solid ground."

"I wouldn't help anyone build a lighthouse even if I *wasn't* sick," he grumbled petulantly. "And I'll believe we'll reach land when we get there. I dun't know why I'm sick, anyway. I never was on the *Maid o' Moidart*."

"Is that your uncle's boat?" A brief nod answered her, and she continued thoughtfully. "I knew he was a fisherman. Maybe he doesn't sail as far out as the *Basset*?"

"He sails far enough," Lewis said, but the brief spurt of energy seemed to have faded. He leaned back against his cushions, eyelids drooping pathetically. "Sebastian says I'm sick just because I dun't want to be here, or dun't think I deserve to be here, or some such."

Emily considered the idea. Seasick because one didn't want to be at sea? It *was* an explanation of sorts, she supposed. "I like Sebastian. I don't know him as well as I do Archimedes—he's been too busy taking care of you—but the few times I've spoken with him, he seemed awfully kind."

"Yeah," Lewis said distantly. His face had gone even paler, which she wouldn't have thought was possible. "He is. I like him, too. Mostly. Oh, glory . . ."

He bolted for the rail and didn't make it. Fortunately, a gremlin holding a bucket appeared out of nowhere. Lewis fell to his knees and retched.

"You aren't throwing up very much anymore," Emily said, examining him. "Just dry heaving. Is that a good sign?"

"No," he gasped, between heaves. "'Tis just—nothin' comes up if nothin' goes down."

"Well, you have to be eating *something*," she said, much disturbed at the implications of his statement. "You'll make yourself ill if you don't."

"I *am* ill. Ahh . . ."

"Oh, dear, not again." Sebastian hurried up, white whiskers waggling in perturbation. "Such a stubborn boy it is, to be sure. I thought we'd be past the worst of it by now. *Tsk, tsk.*"

Lewis retched again, more weakly.

"Land ho!" a voice shouted from aloft. Bosun Eli was leaning out of the crow's nest, wildly waving a spyglass, surrounded by bouncing, cheering gremlins on every spar. "Ahoy! Captain! Land ho!"

Startled, Emily shaded her eyes to see for herself. She'd been so intent on Lewis, and on her calculations before that, she hadn't realized what else was going on, but there was definitely a solid smudge of darker blue against the blue of the waves, just where water should meet sky. Land, for a certainty. Their destination? It looked like an island. . . .

"We've arrived," she told Lewis, feeling her heart begin to beat a little faster. "Look! There's land!"

"Thank you, Saint Piran," he said devoutly, casting one quick, desperate glance at the horizon. Then he stuck his head back in the bucket.

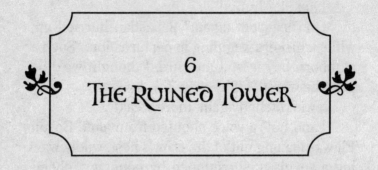

6
The Ruined Tower

Lewis had never been so glad to reach land in his life. Any land, even a strange island in the middle of nowhere.

Solid ground, he thought, shivering and clinging to the railing with both hands. If he'd dared—if he'd thought he was strong enough to make it—he'd have leapt over the side and swum the last few lengths to shore. Beneath him, the deck of the *Basset* rolled gently, and his stomach rolled in response. *At last, at last.*

It seemed he'd been sick for years—but the end was in sight. Maybe soon he'd even be able to eat something that *stayed* eaten for longer than a quarter hour. . . .

The *Basset* was sailing into a peaceful, half-moon-shaped cove lined with sandy beaches. Tall palm trees dotted the shoreline. As the ship tacked smoothly around the point, a silent city came into view, a city of golden stone houses with red-tile roofs. The windows were shuttered or boarded up, and sand piled in drifts against the walls, but the city itself was still strangely lovely—a dream of vanished peace and beauty drowsing in the warm afternoon sun.

But it wasn't the city that drew Lewis's eye— anyone's eye, he thought—it was what loomed behind the city, lifting against the horizon. Rising serenely from the crest of a mountain was an immense tower. Fashioned of gigantic blocks of the same golden stone as the city, it soared into the sky until it seemed to reach almost to the edge of heaven.

Lewis couldn't help it: his jaw dropped, and he stared. *That thing must be over a hundred feet tall!*

The base was square, with broken statues at the corners—a lion, an eagle, and a man with wings on the three corners he could see. They must be huge, Lewis realized, for him to be able to make out any details at all from this distance. Above the statues, the tower was octagonal, its eight sides tapering slightly upward in a great, shining sweep of stone.

The very top was a ruin. Black streaks cut jaggedly across it from a gaping hole in the roof. Only one thing could cause damage like that,

Lewis knew: a fire. A fire hot enough to burn stone. . . .

"Oh!" Off a few feet to one side, Emily Alexander uttered a little gasp and clutched at her father, who was standing next to her. James Alexander had come on deck just after land had been sighted, though for the life of him Lewis couldn't understand why. It wasn't as though he could *see* anything. Even this. "Papa, there's a tower. . . ."

"Yes," James Alexander said, sounding queerly exalted. "A tower. *The* tower."

As if it were the only one that had ever been built. *Well, maybe he has the right of it,* Lewis thought, shaken. *I've certainly never seen anything like it before.*

"Look alive, the harbor!" Captain Malachi was shouting, leaning out over the *Basset*'s railing. "Ahoy, Pharos!"

"Ahoy, Captain!" Answering the hail was a dwarf with a pointed beard, waving from shore. He was surrounded by a small group of excitedly jittering gremlins, obviously part of the *Basset*'s crew. "Ahoy, ahoy!"

"Seaman Augustus," the Captain remarked almost offhandedly. "We left him here on Pharos to begin work while we went off to find you, Mr. Engineer."

Pharos. So that was the name of the island.

Lewis tasted it in the privacy of his mind and shrugged. Any port in a storm.

"But the tower, Papa," Emily was saying, clinging to her father's arm. "What happened to it? Why is it all—all burned like that?"

She sounded frightened. Lewis cast her a curious glance, wondering why the idea of fire should unnerve her so. The thing was a lighthouse, wasn't it? And lighthouses caught fire occasionally, struck by lightning in bad storms. Everyone knew that.

"There was a fire, miss," Sebastian said seriously, looking from her to the tower and back again. "Caused by those who didn't love the light—who didn't believe. Because of it, all this great city of Heliopolis has been abandoned for almost five hundred years ... until this very summer."

"Heliopolis." James Alexander's head lifted alertly. "Hmm."

He sounded as though he knew the name, though how he could, Lewis had no idea. Neither had Emily, to judge by the quick, questioning glance she gave her father—but then the *Basset* was tying up at a small wooden dock that jutted out into the cove, and all such considerations seemed completely beside the point. Land!

Almost before the gangplank was lowered, Lewis had staggered step by weaving step off the

Basset onto the splintered half-timbers of the dock, and then off the end of the dock onto the island. He fell on his knees in the sand, with Sebastian hovering worriedly over him.

"Thank you, Saint Piran," he moaned, conscious of nothing but the fact that neither the ground nor his stomach was rolling anymore. "I swear, I am never goin' to go on another ship as long as I live. Never, never, *never* again."

"Don't be silly," Emily said, stepping daintily down the gangplank with her father. "You'll have to sail home on the *Basset,* at least. Unless you mean to spend the rest of your life on this island. Do you?"

He glared up at her. "Of course I dun't. I just—hey!" A big purple bird with a heron's skinny legs and long neck was standing in front of him. It flapped its wings, and a shower of sparks flew from its feathers. Lewis scrambled to his feet. "That thing's on fire!"

Sebastian chuckled. "It's only a benu bird, lad. Mind the feathers. That's where the sparks are coming from."

Lewis didn't need telling twice. Prudently, he edged backward. The benu bird's long neck curved around, one bright blue eye following his every move.

"Oh, how pretty!" Emily said, delighted. She would be. "Papa, they're like fireworks birds."

"A good description, my dear," her father said, patting her hand fondly. "I can smell the sulfur from here."

So could Lewis. He batted halfheartedly at a few stray sparks, then gave up in disgust. *Fireworks birds. What next?*

"Wonder how one'd taste roasted," he grumbled.

"Oh, we couldn't eat the benu," Sebastian said reprovingly. "They're the guardians of the island. Now, why don't I make you a nice bowl of gruel to settle your stomach? We've a great deal of work to do by Midsummer's Eve. . . ."

That was an understatement, as it turned out. For all that Lewis had had a vague idea that they were sailing someplace to build a lighthouse—not one like this! He hadn't known they could *build* lighthouses like this—he'd mostly been too preoccupied with his stomach to think about it much. Now it was as though nothing mattered to anyone except that incredible tower, and getting it repaired and functioning again by Midsummer's Eve. That made sense for Emily's father, he supposed, and even for Emily, since she was his daughter, but for the whole crew of the *Basset*?

They started to work immediately. Emily and her father settled themselves in the ship's library, reading and sketching and taking notes, while the rest of the crew cut and hauled stone and built frames. Augustus and the gremlins who had been left on the island had already quarried quite a few of the blocks needed for repairs, but it all had to be dressed and laid and mortared into place.

"We'll finish repairs to the base first, for safety's sake," James Alexander decreed. "Then the interior stair, so we can reach the lantern— the area at the top, where the lamp will rest— more easily. Only after *that* will we worry about mounting the lamp itself."

"As you say, Mr. Engineer," Captain Malachi said cheerfully, not seeming to mind a bit that he was following the directions of a blind man. "You're the one who knows how these things are done."

Lewis couldn't understand it—but then, nothing they were doing made a great deal of sense to him. Why did they have to finish by midsummer? Well, he supposed the work had to be finished by some date, and Midsummer's Eve was as good as any—but who needed a lighthouse way out here in the middle of an empty ocean, anyway? No one, that was who.

He said as much to Sebastian, who only smiled.

"We all need light to see by, lad," he said. "And a lighthouse is a brighter light than most.

Are you sure you don't want to help?"

"I'm sure," he said shortly, not wanting to say more. Sebastian had been good to him on the voyage, but catch Lewis dragging stones from a hole in the ground and then all the way up a mountain! And to rebuild a lighthouse, too, when everyone knew that even ordinary lighthouses—never mind this great monster—were foolish wastes of time and money. *Dad would have a fit,* he thought. Let alone what his cousins would say if they ever heard about it. "I've got better things to do."

Only—he didn't, really, he found out in fairly short order.

Days passed. Lewis's relief over his deliverance from seasickness lasted little more than a single one of them. At first, he was grateful just to be able to keep his head out of the bucket and his breakfast in his stomach, where it belonged. Then, as he got his strength back, he began to understand the full extent of what had happened to him—of what had been done to him.

I was kidnapped! he realized indignantly. *Kidnapped and taken to the most boring island in the whole world.*

Boring, and empty. The weather was always the same: warm and sunny, with clear skies. There were no houses, no shops, no market to wander around—no people at all to visit with. No hunting or fishing, either. He couldn't bring himself to ask the loan of one of the *Basset*'s boats to try taking a net out into the cove, and the only animals he'd seen on shore were those silly benu birds. He didn't want to risk offending Sebastian by hunting *them*. Besides, he wasn't sure what sort of sling he'd use on a bird with feathers that lit fires.

By the morning of the tenth day on Pharos, Lewis was going out of his mind with boredom.

"There's nothing to do around here," he told Sebastian defiantly. "I'm going for a walk."

He was half hoping to be contradicted and *ordered* to help work on the tower. He couldn't be blamed or laughed at for doing useless work if he had been ordered, now, could he? Even Zach would have to understand that. And he did owe Sebastian—or someone—for his passage home, even if he hadn't wanted to come in the first place.

But the white-bearded dwarf did no such thing.

"You do that, lad," he said instead, not even looking up from the wooden tub full of mortar he was mixing for tuck-pointing the new stones. "It will be good exercise for you. Don't go too far, though. There's dark places on this island. . . ."

"Dark places? On *this* island?" Lewis snorted. He'd never seen so much sun. Even under the trees there was scarcely more than a hint of shadow. "Yeah. All right. I'll be careful."

I'll go exploring, he decided then and there. *Starting with what's on the other side of the tower.*

But the tower was huge—even vaster than he'd realized. It took him nearly half an hour, by the height of the sun, to walk only two sides of the square base, and by that time he was seriously wishing he'd never begun. Only the fact that it would be just as far going back as going on kept him from returning to the *Basset* in exhaustion.

The sun was so warm that he stripped off his jacket and carried it over one arm—he'd have abandoned it entirely, only it was one of Zach's that Mum had made over for him, and he didn't want her to think he didn't appreciate all her work. And anyway, it was *his* jacket. Emily and her father had had new clothes waiting for them on the *Basset,* but Lewis hadn't wanted any. Though Sebastian had said there was plenty for him, too, he hadn't liked to take advantage of the offer. They might be poor, he and his mother, but they weren't beggars.

Nor ever will be, he thought, loosening his shirt collar. *Glory, but it's hot.* Maybe he ought to find a place in the shade to sleep for a while. If he could find any shade. The light of the noonday sun beat down on him like fire. The skinny palm trees scarcely cast a shadow—what a waste they were. Like everything else on this island. Little sparkles danced in front of his eyes, making him blink—and then, suddenly, there *was* a shadow blocking his way, a dark blot against the golden stone of the tower. *What's that?*

It was a statue carved of some dark stone, shiny black like obsidian. Some sort of bird, he thought, only with scales in place of feathers. The tail was broken. Could it have fallen from higher up the tower? That seemed likely, though he didn't think it was quite as large as the huge statues at the four corners of the base. Craning his neck upward, he tried to decide how far it might have fallen. Not too far, he thought; it wasn't that much damaged. *Wonder how Mr. Engineer and the dwarves are going to get this bit back into place.*

The burned part of the tower wasn't nearly so noticeable from this angle. Perhaps the fallen statue wouldn't need to be replaced. The carving certainly wasn't very attractive ... sort of silly-looking, really, almost like a giant chicken. It would be a pity to waste that shiny black stuff it was carved out of, though. He'd never seen stone polished to such a high gloss before—almost like glass. Perhaps it could be recarved into something else? Curious, he touched the gleaming surface with the tip of one finger.

"Squawk!" With a rush of sparking feathers and the strong smell of sulfur, a benu bird appeared out of nowhere to peck viciously at his extended hand.

"Ouch!" he said, yanking the hand back and shaking it against the sting. "Stop that! I wasn't hurting anything."

Maybe it thought he was going to steal something. Blue eyes darting, the bird hopped away, and then stood on one leg, still watching him intently. Lewis made a face at it.

"I was just touching it," he said, annoyed. Deliberately, he reached out to run his whole hand over the stone. "Why, it's cold. . . ."

More than cold; freezing. His hand—his whole *arm*—shook with a sudden chill, as if he'd plunged it into ice water. But the statue was sitting right in the sun! Stone should absorb heat, not give off cold. Intrigued, he leaned closer. The carving was really very detailed; he could see every scale. And the broken bit, there at the end—it was smooth and polished, too, not broken at all! The tail simply curved *under* the bird shape, toward the ground. Just behind it—set right into the base of the tower—was a small, square panel carved of the same black stone as the statue. A door? Perhaps that was where the cold came from, though he'd be blessed if he could see how or why.

Fascinated, he knelt to run his fingers around the edges of the square, searching for a handle. Yes, it was a door, all right—a trapdoor, embedded in the side of the tower. It had hinges, though no keyhole that he could see. But if it was a door, then it had to open. . . .

"*Squaaawk!*" the benu bird called again from behind him, its croak a rising, urgent wail. "*Squawk-squawk-squeeawk!*"

"Oh, hush yer noise," Lewis told it in irritation. "This is interesting." The most interesting thing he'd seen since he'd landed on this boring island. If he could only—ah! "There, that's done it! I knew there had to be a handle."

The door gave slightly. Shifting his weight to lean forward, he struggled to pull it open. But it wouldn't budge.

And then, all at once and without so much as a creak, the door opened *inward.* Lewis grabbed wildly for something to steady himself against— too late! His questing hands found only smooth stone, nothing to get a grip on, and the weight of his own leaning precipitated him wildly forward. "*Nooo!*"

For an instant, he teetered on the brink. Then, with a headlong rush, he tumbled forward and down, out of the daylight—

—and into a long, echoing darkness.

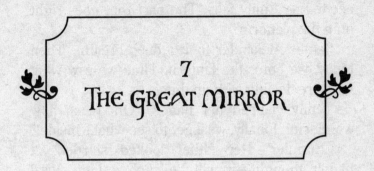

7
The Great Mirror

At first, no one realized that Lewis had disappeared.

"He went for a walk," Sebastian reported when James Alexander asked—as he did every morning—how the boy was faring. "He'll probably be back in time for dinner."

The old dwarf sounded sad. Emily felt sorry for Sebastian, but she didn't really want to waste time thinking about Lewis and his problems. Today was the day they were going to climb all the way to the top of the tower—after all their hard work!

"We've done all we can to shore up the interior," her father had decided just that morning. "Seaman Augustus, you say that the railing has been replaced all the way up?"

"Aye, sir, except for that little bit right at the

top," Augustus replied, sounding almost as excited as Emily felt. "The part that goes right onto the platform."

James Alexander took a deep breath. "Then today, we enter the lantern. Time we saw what we were dealing with up there. . . ."

Emily clapped her hands. "Oh, Papa, how wonderful! Finally, we'll get to see what's inside!"

"Emmie?" Her father looked startled. "I hadn't thought—it will be such a long, hard climb. Are you sure you wouldn't rather wait below, at least for now?"

Her heart fell, but before she could say anything, Captain Malachi spoke up. "Now, Mr. Engineer, I'm sure Miss Emily is just as curious as all the rest of us, and has done just as much work, too. No harm in letting her take a look *with* the rest of us."

"Well, no, I suppose not," James Alexander said. His daughter breathed a sigh of relief and nodded gratefully to the *Basset*'s captain.

It *was* a long climb. They went up the base of the tower first, her father, Archimedes, Captain Malachi, and Seaman Augustus. And Emily, accompanied by several gremlins. Even the benu birds seemed excited; they lighted the little party's way into the tower with their clashing, sparking feathers, flying gracefully up and down the vast interior. Inside, the shadows were long, and dust motes sparkled in the beams of light from the slit windows placed at the landings. Emily strained as she trudged up stair after stair after stair, trying to see to the very top—but it was no use.

"Stay close to the wall," Augustus warned, nervously shooing her away from the newly repaired railing. "It's a long way down."

The interior of the tower was musty with age. Once, there had been frescoes painted on the walls, bright scenes of birds in flight and palm trees and seascapes, but the colors had faded to almost nothing. Emily trailed one hand across them as she walked, feeling the paint and plaster flake away beneath her fingers.

How old this place is, she thought, awed. *Older than old. . . .*

Up and up and up they went, past the first window, which her father stopped to inspect. "The glass is warped and will need to be replaced," he commented, running his hand carefully along the broken frame; Captain Malachi only nodded. The second window had no glass at all, only a benu bird roosting on the sill. Sebastian had called them the guardians of the island; now Emily wondered if they were guarding the tower as well. But against what?

Up still more stairs, spiraling dizzily into the sky. The last stretch was the hardest. Gradually, the landings disappeared and the staircase turned into a true spiral, winding through the narrowing tower. They didn't stop at all for that part, not even for a moment. Emily's legs ached, and her lungs felt as if she'd been breathing dust for hours, but she refused to complain. If she did, her father might regret having brought her.

And then, just when she thought she'd have to give up and ask for a pause to catch her breath, they were there, in a small room at the very top of the tower: the lantern, where the lighthouse lamp would eventually be mounted. But it wasn't really a room—it had no walls, only eight stone pillars evenly spaced around the edges, just inside a protective ledge. The whole place was open to the sky. Benu birds roosted all around the edges and on top of the pillars, look- ing in with bright, curious eyes. They were oddly silent and still, with not a single spark or ruffled purple feather showing.

Emily stopped abruptly, waiting for her eyes to adjust to the sudden return to out-of-doors. She wanted to be sure to see everything clearly, in case her father asked her about it later. But there wasn't all that much to see. Everything on the platform was black from an ancient fire, the very rock underfoot all crazed and crackled from the heat—

Except for the object in the very center, a

shining, concave silver disk about half again the height of a grown man. It was glowing softly, giving off a rose-gold light visible even against the brightness of day.

It looks like a giant's silver punch bowl, she thought, trying to look at it straight on without blinking. *Why isn't it burned, too?*

"The Great Mirror of the sun," Malachi said simply. "The Light of Pharos."

"Hmm. Yes." James Alexander knelt and ran knowledgeable fingers over the surface of the Mirror. Its sheer size seemed to surprise him, and he took his time. "It's warm."

"It holds the heat of the day," Archimedes said from beside him. "Then at night, the light shines. . . ."

"A fixed beam?"

"Fixed facing east," Captain Malachi said from his other side.

James Alexander nodded, as if he'd been expecting some such response. Again, Emily got the impression, as she had several times since they'd come to Pharos, that her father knew more than he was saying. "What range?"

"Um—about ten leagues," Archimedes answered, with a strangely uneasy glance at the captain. Malachi nodded reassuringly at his helmsman. "Perhaps a little farther, on especially clear nights and when the world is holding still."

When the world is holding still—what does he mean by that? Emily thought. She waited for her father to ask, but he didn't.

"About thirty miles, then," he said, standing and dusting off his hands. "Impressive. Yes, I think I can make it work again, as it used to. But we'll never get a reflector of this weight to flash without a proper lens."

"We don't need it to flash," Captain Malachi said, smiling and heaving an obvious sigh of relief at the engineer's conclusion. "Just so the light is shining to the east on Midsummer's Eve. . . ."

James Alexander went very still. Emily held her breath. What was Malachi talking about? Even she knew better than that—even Lewis would have, if he'd been there. A lighthouse that needed to be lit for only one night of the year made no sense at all.

"I wondered," her father said softly. "I did wonder. Especially when Cassandra and Edmund wouldn't say . . . Captain Malachi, I think it's about time you answered a few questions."

"Questions, sir?" The *Basset*'s captain was guarded. "What questions?"

"About the *Basset*'s need for a lighthouse, for one," James Alexander said crisply, every inch an engineer. "Really, Captain. Archimedes was most helpful in explaining the workings of your marvelous *wuntarlabe* to me so I could use it to get the readings I wanted—but I doubt that when he did so he realized that *I* would then see just how unnecessary a lighthouse is for a vessel so equipped. The *Basset* will never be lost at sea— not with its *wuntarlabe* to guide it."

Emily blinked. *What does he mean?* She'd known that the *wuntarlabe* was a remarkable instrument—as remarkable as the *Basset* and her crew—but still . . .

"There *are* other ships," Malachi offered, as if he, at least, understood quite well. "Or there may be other ships, one day."

"In *these* waters?" James Alexander shook his head decisively. "Not likely. Come, Captain, let's have no more games. I've known since the day we set sail that we were embarking on a . . . rather unusual voyage. Into the realm of ancient myth, perhaps? After all, I'd just accepted a commission to rebuild the lighthouse at Pharos, one of the long-lost Wonders of the Ancient World! But the tower is here, as promised, and the Great Mirror is here, gathering its light by no known scientific agency—and I find that I do resent being taken for a fool."

A tense little silence fell across the platform. Suddenly frightened, Emily moved closer to her father, frantically wishing his last words unsaid. If Captain Malachi took offense . . . For the first time it occurred to her just how far they were from Cornwall, and how alone. *Oh, Papa, don't. Let them have their secrets.*

Then the captain laughed, and the tension melted away as if it had never been.

"The realm of myth, eh, Mr. Engineer?" he said, chuckling and shaking his head admiringly. "The Lands of Legend, *we'd* say. I should have known you'd see deeper into a millstone than most. You'd do well at the College of Magical Knowledge, you would. You might consider applying for a faculty position there one day."

"One day, perhaps," James Alexander said gruffly, apparently pleased by the compliment but not at all distracted. Emily's heart swelled with pride. "Now, will you answer my question? Or would I be right in simply assuming that the light is needed as a signal?"

Malachi chuckled again. "As a signal, aye. Do you want to know to whom? Or have you already worked out the answer to that question, too?"

"Hmm." James Alexander stared outward, blind eyes seeing something no one else could. "A light that shines east on the eve of the summer solstice—once every five hundred years, perhaps?" Malachi nodded involuntarily; James Alexander couldn't see the gesture, but evidently he didn't need to. "Yes. Yes, I suspect I do know the answer to that question, too, Captain." He

took a deep breath. "Now, since we *are* facing
the deadline of finishing by midsummer—and
since Midsummer's Eve *is* only a week away—
we'd best get back to work. The next step is a
mounting for the Mirror. Stone, I believe. Wood
wouldn't be strong enough to hold that weight
for long. Perhaps the gremlins could carve something suitable out of granite. . . ."

"Yes, sir," Malachi said, eyes twinkling.
Again, he seemed to understand perfectly.

Emily certainly didn't, though she was happy
that her father was satisfied. But she couldn't get
anyone to explain.

"Figure it out for yourself," her father
said imperturbably when she asked him. "It
shouldn't be difficult for one with your educa-
tional background."

And when she tried to ask Archimedes privately what her father and Captain Malachi had
been talking about, the *Basset*'s helmsman
wouldn't tell her, either.

"A very well-read man, your father is, Miss
Emily," was all he would say—though he said it
very respectfully. "Very well-read, indeed."

It was not until dinner that night, camped at
the base of the tower—James Alexander had
wanted to take some more measurements before
returning to the *Basset* for the evening—that
Emily realized someone was missing.

"Where's Lewis?" she asked, glancing around. "He never misses a meal."

Sebastian looked startled. "Why, so he doesn't. I hadn't thought—Eli, has he been back to the ship this afternoon?"

"No, not at all," the bosun said. He'd been standing watch on the *Basset* most days while the rest of them worked on the tower. "I haven't seen him since breakfast."

"Oh, dear, oh, dear—Captain?"

"We'll have to look for him," Malachi said, his genial features taking on a grim cast. "Search parties, two and two, each with a lantern and a whistle. And step lively, all of you—night's coming on."

"Do you think something's happened to him?" James Alexander asked worriedly.

Emily could have screamed. Her father had been so happy, so confident, and now this! *He* couldn't help search for Lewis, and it would make him feel awful and useless and *blind* again. He felt *responsible* for Lewis, though she was sure he shouldn't. If that horrid boy truly had gotten lost, then she was certain it was his own fault.

"I don't know, Mr. Engineer," Malachi said, equally worried. "We'll have to see what we can find."

What they found was Lewis's jacket, around the back of the tower. "Just lying on the ground next to the black statue, it was, Captain," Archimedes reported, holding out the rough tweed for their inspection. It was Lewis's jacket, all right: no one else on the *Basset* wore anything made-over. "No signs of any struggle."

"Statue? What statue?" James Alexander said sharply. "One of those from the tower?"

"Not the tower exactly . . . ," Malachi temporized. Then he shrugged. "Ah, well, best we face facts. Where there is light, Mr. Engineer, there is always darkness. And since we mean to summon one of the great beings of light back to the Lands of Legend, it's only to be expected that one of the beings of darkness would return as well. It's the statue of the Basilisk that Archimedes is referring to, around the back and bottom of the tower where it belongs. Young Lewis must have found it on his rambles."

"Poor lad, poor lad," Sebastian sighed, shaking his head. "He believed, right enough, but he still couldn't see. . . ."

"A basilisk!" James Alexander sounded taken aback. "You mean—a cockatrice? Half rooster, half serpent?"

"And all evil," Malachi said grimly. "I wouldn't call *the* Basilisk by that name, though, were I you and chanced to meet him. He thinks it's an insult."

"But what would a cockatrice—sorry,

basilisk—want with a boy like Lewis?"

"Now, that I couldn't say," the *Basset*'s captain said heavily. "We'd best keep a close watch on the *Basset* by night, though, until we find out. The benu birds are almost blind in the darkness."

"Is there danger?" Looking alarmed, James Alexander reached out one hand, groping. "Emily? Emmie, where are you?"

"Right here, Papa," she said, taking his hand reassuringly.

"There's no danger, sir," Sebastian spoke up, sounding sad again. "Or at least—not to us. As for young Lewis . . ."

Silence fell. Holding tightly to her father's hand, Emily tried to be angry at Lewis again— after all, it *was* his own fault he'd gone wandering off—but she found that she couldn't, quite. Night was very dark on the island, she realized, thinking of being away from the comfort and safety of the *Basset*. To be all alone in the blackness of that night, and lost . . . Wherever the Aldestow boy was now, she hoped he was all right.

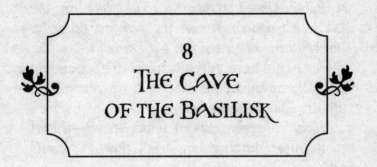

8
THE CAVE
OF THE BASILISK

Lewis woke slowly, his head throbbing fit to split. He was lying flat on his back against solid rock. A painful lump of stone was digging into his spine right between his shoulder blades, and his whole body ached. When he opened his eyes, he thought for a horrified moment he was blind, like Emily's father—but then he blinked and realized the truth.

It's dark in here.

Wherever "here" was. Dark, and cold, and dank. As his eyes adjusted, he determined he was in a cave so vast that he could scarcely make out the end of it. Sickly, phosphorescent green goo covered the walls closest to him and dripped down from above, providing what little light there was; the air was close and . . . musky, sort of. Peculiar and unpleasant.

Not a nice place at all, this wasn't. *How did I get here? Oh—I remember. The door in the wall . . . a <u>trapdoor</u>. It sure trapped me, all right. That benu tried to warn me, but I didn't listen.*

He should have. Already missing his jacket in the chilly dimness, he tried to lever himself up onto his elbows to see better.

"Hsss!" A scaly, clawed hand—paw?—thrust at his chest, forcing him back down. *"Nasssty* boy."

"Huh? What—what are—" *A lizard,* he realized dumbly, staring. A lizard almost the height of a grown man, with a pointed snout and a thick tail that twitched behind its squarish body. Claws flexed cruelly against Lewis's shirt, lightly piercing the skin beneath. "Don't—you're hurting me! Let me go—"

"Heh-heh-heh." Hissing and laughter, echoing all around. *"Sss . . ."*

He was in the middle of a *crowd* of lizards, Lewis saw with horror—dozens of them. Hundreds! Mottled scales and spines and claws stirred in the shadows, encircling him. All different sizes and colors, too. The one closest to him had black-and-gray scales, with bumps all over that looked like warts; behind him crouched a muddy green-and-brown one with a swollen tumor on its snout. A third was smaller, with a series of bent spines running down its back and only a stump where its left foreleg should have been, while a fourth was missing an eye and kept turning its head back and forth in an effort to see him.

They were all amazingly ugly. And they smelled—rotten, sort of. Like meat or milk gone bad in the sun, and stinking. He swallowed, trying not to be ill.

"You come with the benu, nasssty boy," said the first lizard, opening its mouth to reveal a double row of very sharp teeth. Its forked tongue flickered. "No more. You sssseek the cave of the Basssilisk?"

"No!" Frantic, he struggled to escape. What did the creature mean, "basilisk"? "I was just— just explorin'. I dun't—I wasn't seekin' nothin'!"

"You lie, boy." The triangular snout bent closer, mouth gaping. Lewis flinched, pulling his face away from the fetid breath. "Sssalamanders sssay you lie. . . . *King Basssilisk* sssays you lie."

"I dun't lie, you—" A salamander was a kind of lizard, he knew that, but he'd never heard of one this big before. Or of lizards that talked, even hissing. But then, before he'd sailed on the *Basset,* he'd never heard of herons with purple feathers that lit fires, either. "I dun't know any basilisk. I fell down a hole in the wall, that's all. I just fell down a hole!"

"You comes with the makesss-lightsss,

nasssty, nasssty," the green-and-brown salamander said, circling behind his head. Lewis twisted frantically, trying to accomplish the impossible feat of seeing behind his own back while lying flat on the floor. "The buildsss-tallsss . . ."

Makes-lights . . . builds-talls . . . It means the lighthouse! "I do not!" he said, choking the words out. "I dun't like lighthouses. I wouldn't help build one if I knew how. Ask anyone!"

More hissing, still malicious, but slightly confused. The tightening circle of lizard bodies pulled back slightly, and Lewis shuddered with relief. They believed him. Maybe they would let him go . . . but then a shadow fell between the crowd of salamanders and the greenish glow on the wall—a shadow taller and more massive than any of the lizards. The salamanders cringed, their bellies flat against the ground.

"Bring him," a deep voice said from just beyond Lewis's sight.

Eagerly, the salamanders obeyed. Clawed hands yanked him ungently to his feet, pinching as well as pushing. "Oww!"

"Be sssilentsss!" the black-and-gray salamander hissed.

But the owner of the deep voice had heard. "A cry of pain . . . so long since We have heard a cry of human pain in these halls. Are you injured, mortal child?"

"N-no," Lewis stuttered. *Who does he think he's callin' a child?*

"Good. We would not wish you to be so injured in Our halls. . . ."

There was a sound of scales sliding against stone, and a—a *thing* black as the midnight sky without stars slithered into sight. It was more than twice as tall as Lewis, with its top half resembling an enormous rooster, only covered with snakeskin instead of feathers. A rooster's comb sat flabbily on top of the huge head, while cock's wattles hung down below the beak.

Below, the thing was a snake. A tail easily three times the thickness of a grown man's leg coiled and twisted behind the rooster's body as if it had a mind of its own. Chicken legs hung down from the front, twitching as they dragged along the floor, and stubby wings flapped awkwardly on either side of the creature; only the tail seemed to provide any reliable means of locomotion.

The most horrible thing was that Lewis recognized it immediately. *The statue,* he thought sickly. *It's the statue come to life.*

How could he ever have thought the carving was silly-looking? The reality was anything but silly. It was—monstrous.

"Look upon Us," the creature said, lowering its glittering eyes. One rooster claw reached out and grabbed Lewis by the shirtfront, dragging him closer. "Look upon Us, and tremble with mortal awe. *We* are *Basilisk*!"

"Y-yes, sir," Lewis stuttered. So the monster was called "Basilisk"? It lifted him clear off of the floor in a single easy motion, so that he was nose to, well, nose with that wicked-looking beak. He bit his tongue, willing himself not to cry out. Somehow, he knew that a show of weakness or fear would not be a good idea, any more than it would have been when facing his bullying cousins. "S-sir. Um—could you put me down now, please, Mr. Basilisk, sir? Please? I can—I can look at you just as easy from the ground, I'm sure. . . ."

"So-o . . ." Gently, the claws flexed, slowly lowering him to the ground. Released, Lewis fell to his knees as his legs flatly refused to support him. Behind him, the semicircle of salamanders hissed and whispered, vaguely threatening. "You claim to be one who hates the light—truth?"

The head whipped around to fix him with a glittering black eye—a snake's eye in a cock's skull.

"Well, I—I—" Put that way, it sounded wrong. Lewis squirmed. *I dun't hate the light, do I? Not really.* But— "I dun't like lighthouses, sir, an' that's a fact. Mr. Basilisk, sir. They're a hardship to honest men, my dad says. An' unnatural, too."

"You understand," the Basilisk said, nodding

regally. Its wattles quivered comically, but Lewis
felt not the slightest inclination to laugh. "You are
the one We have waited for, these long years . . .
the mortal who will free Us, as the legend foretold."

"What legend?" Lewis blurted out. Did the
thing always call itself "We"? Wait a minute—the
gray-and-black salamander had said "King
Basilisk." The Queen off in London used "We,"
he knew. So maybe if the monster really was king
of the salamanders, it had a right. "What do I
understand?"

"You *understand* that the light is the enemy of
these, Our poor subjects." One dangling claw
waved negligently at the crouching salamanders.
"As it is the enemy of you and yours. And as for
the legend—long and long have We waited for
your appearance, mortal boy. . . ."

"Is—is that why you burned the tower?"
Lewis asked timidly. "Because you got tired of
waiting?"

The Basilisk reared back, comb rising like an
angry rooster's. "Who told you We burned the
tower? For half a thousand years the tower has
been dark, and We had no cause to burn it. We
break no ancient laws!"

"No one told me," Lewis gasped. A deep frus-
tration as well as rage filled the Basilisk's tones;
somehow, Lewis had the feeling that the monster

would have liked to burn the tower, but didn't dare. "I didn't—I just thought—well, *someone* burned it, an' you're so powerful an' a king an' all. . . ."

"Ah, yes. We perceive. . . . It is a logical mortal." The Basilisk almost purred, if a snake could purr. Slowly, the comb went flat. "And yet—it is not the tower that must be destroyed, but the Great Mirror."

"The mirror, sir?" he ventured timidly. *What mirror? What's he talkin' about?* It didn't seem wise to ask. "Why?"

"The Mirror gathers the sun's light by day and burns by night," the Basilisk told him, bending forward. The cock's head turned from side to side, regarding him first with one eye and then with the other. "That light is poison to these poor salamanders, who can bear any fire but that of the sun. On their own, they cannot resist its power. But you—*you* will bring *Us* with them into the tower, past the guardian birds whose fires are as deadly as the sun, who threaten salamanders but never mortals. With your aid—as the legend foretold—We will destroy the Great Mirror!"

Guardian birds? It must mean the benu. Sebastian had called them guardians. . . . Salamanders pressed closely around Lewis, their scaly bodies giving off a bone-chilling cold that was worse than the smell. He couldn't think with them so close to him—he could barely breathe.

I've got to do what they want, he reasoned, shivering—from cold, he told himself, though he knew deep down it was really from fear. *They'll kill me, else. Or keep me down here in the dark forever.* The very idea made him want to whimper like a baby—like the baby boy Zach had taunted him with being, a thousand years in the past. Dying might be easier than living forever with salamanders. Besides, what was so dreadful about breaking a mirror? Mirrors were cheap. Even Mum had one.

The memory of his mother decided him. He had to get out of this cave somehow. Whatever it took.

"Yes, sir," he said, wiping sweaty palms on his trousers. "I'll help you break this mirror thing if you want. You just tell me what to do, an' I'll do it."

"Then follow Us, mortal child," the Basilisk commanded, wattles quivering. It didn't seem the least bit surprised or grateful at his agreement, Lewis noticed—more like it had expected him to say yes all along. Around him, the salamanders stirred, hissing and twisting in the shadows. "We will show you the way."

They started by going back up through the cave to the base of the tower through a long, narrow tunnel sloping gently upward, lit by more of that green goo on the walls. Lewis didn't think it was the same way he'd come into the cave—his bruises made him believe he'd fallen more steeply—but it was the way the Basilisk led.

A muttering crowd of salamanders attended their king's every move—and Lewis's. Green-and-Brown seemed especially suspicious, hovering near Lewis every step of the way.

"Hsss," it whispered, its forked tongue flickering unpleasantly close to his ear. "Nasssty, *nasssty."*

No, ol' Green-and-Brown didn't like Lewis at all, that was sure.

I ought to introduce him to Emily, Lewis thought morbidly as the Basilisk paused briefly. He was glad of the moment's respite; the air in the tunnel was getting thick. *They'd get along just fine.*

Which really wasn't fair, he supposed, but he couldn't make himself care. Somehow, his feud with Emily seemed very petty and far away, now that he was trapped in this underground nightmare of lizards and their monster king. He thought longingly of his days on the *Basset,* when the bucket and his griping belly had been all he'd had to fear. In retrospect, even the seasickness hadn't been so bad. . . .

"We arrive," the Basilisk said abruptly, swinging its tail around and knocking a few salamanders backward. The lizards scrambled hastily back to their feet but made no complaint. "Open the gate, mortal child."

"What?" Lewis found himself propelled forward, Green-and-Brown's shove catching him by surprise. "Oh."

They were at the end of the tunnel, facing a large circular slab of black stone set into a wall. Not the door he'd come in by, he was sure—this one was far larger. Basilisk-sized. Gulping, he ducked past those dangling rooster feet and began to feel around for the hinges. If it was built the same way the smaller door had been, he ought to be able to find the catch easily enough.

Wonder why he doesn't open the door himself, he thought as he worked. *Door, gate, whatever it is. Or the salamanders—they've got claws like hands. Maybe they aren't—aren't* handy *enough to jigger it?* Despite the circumstances, he couldn't help a covert snicker at his own pun. The salamanders certainly weren't handy, to judge by the awkward way they pawed at him—or very clever, either, so far as he could tell. And the Basilisk didn't *have* hands. *He did say he needed me—a mortal—to free him. . . .*

That would explain a great deal, it would. He didn't think the Basilisk would like to admit to being imprisoned, or to being helpless. But if the salamanders couldn't get into the tower on their own, and the Basilisk couldn't get out of the tunnel on *his* own, then that was why they needed Lewis. Maybe.

The black slab swung aside silently, revealing the soft, rustling darkness of the underbrush around the tower's base. Lewis breathed in deeply, cleansing his lungs. It was dark outside, with only the stars and a pale sliver of a moon for light, but at least the air was fresh.

"At last," the Basilisk whispered—well, whispered for it. "Free!" Lewis would have been pleased to have his suspicions confirmed, but the Basilisk didn't give him time to consider the matter. Surging forward, it stopped suddenly, halfway through the opening. "Mortal child, if you will betray Us now . . ."

"I won't," Lewis said quickly, stepping back. Did the monster always suspect treachery? "I'll help you break the mirror. I promise."

The chicken's head swung menacingly, wattles waggling. "Then to *you* goes the honor of leading the way."

Wonderful. Lewis swallowed. He didn't want to lead this gang of reptiles anywhere. "Yes, sir. Yer Majesty. Thank you *so* much. . . ."

Did the Basilisk catch the hint of sarcasm? He didn't think so from the way it preened, apparently well pleased by his response. And anyway, it *was* good to be out under the open sky again, even if the salamanders did jostle close. Lewis led them around the side of the tower the way he'd come, hoping that one of the benu birds might stop them. But all the fireworks seemed to be spent for the night.

When they got to the front of the tower, it was deserted. The crescent moon rode high over the harbor, outlining the quiet shape of the *Basset* at her mooring. There were benu birds roosting in the palm trees; one opened a drowsy eye, and then—apparently reassured by what it saw— tucked its head back under its wing.

Fine guardians they were.

"A'right," Lewis said, keeping his voice low. "Follow me."

Through the great front entrance and up the stairs they went, Lewis leading the way like a Pied Piper luring a million lizards—and one huge monster. Though he'd never been inside the tower, he didn't have any doubt about which way he should go: straight up. The very top of a light- house—what had Emily's father called it? the lantern?—was the logical place to find anything important. Especially anything having to do with light, like a burning mirror.

The shaft itself was as dark as the Basilisk's cave, or almost. Here and there, little slit win- dows let in just enough moonlight to cast weird shadows across the curving interior walls. Round and round they went, dizzyingly higher and higher, until it seemed that they might really be climbing all the way to heaven, while the ground fell away beneath them, out of sight. Two circuits of the spiral stair—four—eight. At ten, Lewis stopped counting. He kept his eyes upward and stayed as close to the inner wall as he dared. The stairs seemed to go on forever. About a million miles into the sky, he had to pause to rest.

Dun't like to think about how far is down, he thought, panting and clinging to the railing. *Anyone who fell so far wouldn't leave more than a smear on the bottom.*

"Hey!" Lewis jumped at the sharp, stabbing pain in his side. Green-and-Brown was crouched next to him, all four claws extended. "That hurt!"

"Why are We stopping, mortal child?" the Basilisk boomed from behind, its voice echoing through the tower. "Is the Mirror here?"

"No, sir," Lewis said, a wary eye on the salamander. "Just a little ways more, I reckon."

The green-and-brown salamander showed its teeth in a wide reptilian grin.

Enjoying himself, is he? Lewis thought sourly. *That makes one of us.*

They resumed climbing. The tower was narrower now; he could almost reach out and touch the railing on the other side. Salamander claws made little clicking and scraping noises on the stair treads, covering the soft slithering of the Basilisk's tail. One more circuit of stairs . . .

And then they were at the top, with nothing between them and the stars. Lewis stood aside as the Basilisk squirmed through the opening— for a moment, he thought it wasn't going to fit, but no such luck—and then watched as the salamanders fizzed onto the platform, maliciously delighted. In the exact center of the open space was a large object, shining softly: the Great Mirror.

So that was what it was. . . .

"So-o," the Basilisk breathed. It leaned forward over the silver surface of the Mirror, tongue flickering for all the world as if it wanted to taste the metal. "Lift it. But carefully— carefully! Beware the burning. . . ."

Salamanders swarmed the thing, hissing and shoving as they tugged. Green-and-Brown prodded Lewis expectantly. He was supposed to help, was he? Well, all right. He'd promised. And *he* didn't have to worry about the light. Grunting, he set his knee on the floor behind the Mirror and put his shoulder into it.

Inch by inch, the Mirror lifted, wobbling slightly as the salamanders forced it upward. Once up, it was no trick at all to balance it on its rim—but then it started to glow more brightly. Like the sun brought to earth. . . . The salamanders hissed sharply, pulling back and covering their eyes with their claws, but Lewis stared in awe.

It's beautiful, he thought, dazed. *No one said it would be beautiful.* Likely the salamanders didn't see it that way, he realized, but so it was: beautiful and brilliant. *A light in the darkness . . .*

"Quickly, quickly," the Basilisk hissed, flapping its wings. "Night will not last. To the edge!"

"Huh?" But for once, the command wasn't aimed at Lewis. Salamanders were crawling all over the Mirror again, heads turned away from the light as they shifted it toward the edge of the platform. Metal ground stone with a harsh grating noise. Were they going to tip it over the side? That would break it, all right. But they weren't just moving the Mirror. They were pointing it, outward and down. Aiming it—at the *Basset*! "What are you doing?"

Green-and-Brown hissed at him mockingly, "Nasssty boy. Nasssty, nasssty boy makesss firesss."

But that would mean . . .

"You can't do that," Lewis said in panic. Already light was gathering in the depths of the silver bowl, smoking with heat. The salamanders keened, a wild, savage noise that was half pain, half triumph. "You'll set the ship on fire! You said you were going to break the Mirror—"

"What is broken may be mended, mortal child," the Basilisk said, leaning forward eagerly to watch its subjects work. "But if the Builder, the Maker of Lights—if *he* is destroyed as the Mirror is broken, then all comes surely to naught for this turn of the cycle. Our darkness will rule!"

The Maker of Lights? But—

"You mean Mr. Alexander?" Lewis said, shocked. "He never did anything to you! He was just hired, that's all. You can't—"

The glittering black eyes turned on him. "*We* are Basilisk, foolish mortal. We are *King*!"

"Not my king, you aren't!" Lewis cried, jumping forward. If they set fire to the *Basset,* half the crew would be trapped belowdecks. Emily—Mr. Alexander—Sebastian, who had been so kind to him—even the funny little gremlins—they'd all be burned alive! "No! I won't let you do it!"

"Traitor!" the Basilisk howled, snapping at him. "Would you betray *Us*?"

Its legs shot out, but Lewis ducked away, evading the blow. Wildly, he looked around for a weapon and found a long chisel, probably left in the tower by one of the work crew. Grabbing it, he swung at the nearest salamander, which squalled in outrage. Green-and-Brown was next, scrabbling along the stone with panic as Lewis struck at it.

"Can't take it, can ye," he said, panting

hundreds! But he had to try. "Just like my cousin Zach. Bullies, the whole lot o' ye—"

"Stop him!" The Basilisk's forelegs were dancing and jerking with rage. "The guardians awaken!"

All at once, the tower was full of benu birds, screeching and squawking in anger, their feathers sparking madly. Salamanders fled the fireworks showers in terror.

And about time, too, Lewis thought, swinging the chisel again. The salamanders hissed and fought each other to be first to slither down the stairwell. *Hah. Like rats deserting a sinking ship.*

Lewis crowed. "You lose, Yer Majesty!" Far away, he could hear the *Basset*'s alarm bell, the shouts of the dwarves. "Help's on its way!"

"No!" The Basilisk pecked and flapped furiously, its massive tail twisting and coiling behind it. "We will not fail! We are *Basilisk*!"

Lurching forward, it caught him in a loop of its tail, knocking him off his feet. Then the whole length of it, rooster and snake, was flailing at the base of the Mirror, pushing at it.

"No! Stop!" Lewis cried, scrambling upright. "You'll go over with it!"

Too late. Slowly, inexorably, the silver disk of the Mirror began to turn, rolling toward the edge of the platform. Monster and Mirror teetered briefly, and then, with a horrible, shrieking noise of metal against stone, they fell together. Immediately, the black shadow of the Basilisk separated from the central mass, stubby wings flapping wildly as it disappeared into the night.

The Mirror continued its descent. Like a falling star, it hurtled toward the ground. Shouts drifted up from below, the yammering cries of gremlins and the outraged squawks of benu birds. There was a sound like a bell ringing very far away, and a heartrending, metallic crash.

And then, silence. Even the benu birds were quiet. On shaking legs, Lewis made his way to the edge of the platform and looked down. Far, far below he could see a glint of captured sunlight, a pathetic pile of shards and slivers of silver: the Great Mirror of the sun, shattered beyond repair.

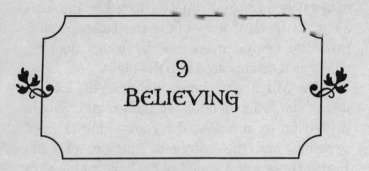

9
BELIEVING

The Mirror was broken. Emily could scarcely believe her eyes as she stared at the jagged pieces of shining silver scattered around the base of the tower, mourning benu birds and gremlins tiptoeing among them sadly. Even shattered, the fragments still glowed within their strange interior light, but the whole magical thing was undeniably ruined—and all because of that awful Lewis Trelawny.

She glared at him angrily where he stood leaning against the side of the tower, watching the sun rise. As if he felt her resentful gaze, he turned to look at her and smiled faintly in resignation. Her mouth tightened. Did he think this was *funny*?

"This is your doing, you know," she whispered to him furiously, while Archimedes and her father inspected the worst of the damage. "If you hadn't wandered off like that, none of this would have happened. I should black your other eye for you—or worse!"

He shrugged, eyes sliding past to the broken bits of metal. "Yeah. You should."

"I hope you're proud of yourself!"

Another shrug. "Dun't much matter now, does it."

Taken aback, she closed her mouth over more angry words. Why wasn't he fighting back? He ought to be saying he hadn't had a choice, that the Basilisk monster she'd glimpsed so briefly from the ship had forced him, or—or pleading for forgiveness, or *something*! Why was the boy just *standing* there like a lump? Almost as if he didn't care . . . but he *had* to care. It was all his fault.

"It's no use," James Alexander said, standing after his inspection of the broken Mirror. His voice was flat—hopeless, Emily thought. As if all the life had been leached out of it. "None of the fragments is large enough to generate a beam of sufficient power."

"Are you certain?" Archimedes said, prodding the largest silver chunk, a jagged, crescent-shaped remnant. "This one seems almost twice the size of the others. . . ."

"No," James Alexander said tiredly. "The

surface area of the largest fragment might be sufficient if we recalculated the focal plane, but it's cracked. Too much direct pressure would only splinter it even further, I'm afraid. That leaves us with no immediate option. Unless the Mirror can be repaired . . ."

"Repaired!" Captain Malachi scowled. "If you can think of a way to do *that,* Mr. Engineer, I'd be glad to hear of it. We've so little time left until the solstice . . ."

"I know. I'm sorry, Captain. I have no further suggestions." He groped for his cane. "Emily?"

"Here, Papa," she said, slipping her hand into the crook of his elbow.

"I would like to return to the ship, please."

"Of course, Papa," she said, frowning slightly. It wasn't like him to ask for her help so directly. *Maybe he wants to see if there is something in the library that might help. There might be a way to— to build a new lamp or something.*

She flinched at the thought. It was building a new lamp that had cost her father his sight. Still, he did know all about lenses and optics and such things . . . more than she did, who had never been truly interested in his work.

But when they approached the *Basset,* James Alexander didn't even acknowledge Sebastian's hail. It was left to Emily to shake her head at the elderly dwarf.

"No chance at all?" Sebastian asked, his face falling. Around him, the rest of the crew clustered hopefully.

"Papa says not," Emily told him honestly, turning troubled eyes to her father as he moved tentatively up the familiar gangplank. He ought to have learned his way around the ship by heart, after all the days spent at sea and on the island. She'd thought he had. "Captain Malachi and Archimedes are doing something with the fragments. Tidying up."

James Alexander didn't say a word until they got belowdecks. Then, when Emily would have led him to the library, he spoke.

"No," he said.

"But, Papa—"

"Take me to my cabin."

Confused and upset, she obeyed, and was left standing in the corridor staring at a closed door.

The door stayed closed all that day and into the evening. He never came out, not even for meals—not even when Captain Malachi and Archimedes returned to the ship.

Finally, Emily could stand it no longer.

I have to go to him, she thought. *I can't just— leave him like this.*

One of the smaller gremlins trailed after her as she went and stood uncertainly in front of the door. She wasn't sure why, but she found that she was glad of the company.

"Papa?" Hesitantly, she rapped. No answer. "Papa, are you in there?"

Foolish question. Where else would he be? Still . . . she tried the doorknob: locked. Now what?

A tug on her skirt made her look down. The gremlin's expression was sober, without a hint of the mischievous expression he and his fellows usually wore. He rummaged around in the crown of his tall hat and pulled out an ornate brass key.

At first she didn't understand. Then she did. "Oh! Is that the key to *this* door?"

A sly nod and an embarrassed scuffling of shoes.

Well, if the gremlin thought she ought to go in . . . She took the key, fitted it into the lock, and turned. The door swung open.

The cabin was dim, illuminated only by the weak twilight filtering through the porthole. Her father was sitting in the chair, his hands lying loosely across his knees, palms up.

"Papa?" she said uncertainly, crossing the room to him. "Why are you sitting here in the dark?"

"Is it dark?" he asked heavily. "I hadn't noticed."

"Well, of course you—yes, it's dark." Groping

for matches, she lit the desk lamp and turned the wick high. "There, that's better. Captain Malachi and Archimedes are back from the tower. I thought you'd want to speak with them."

"What for? There's nothing I can do to help."

He turned his face away, but not before she caught a glimpse of suspicious wetness on his scarred cheek. Had her father been *crying*? No, that was ridiculous. Papa never cried, not even when he was in such pain after the accident. The only time she'd ever seen him shed tears was— was on the day of Mama's funeral. . . .

"Oh, Papa, no!" He was giving up! After all this! Sinking to her knees beside his chair, she clasped his hands in both of hers. "You can't give up now. You know all about lights, and mirrors, and lenses. You can—"

"I *cannot,*" he said harshly, his grip tightening against hers. "Emily, I am blind. I can't design a new lamp for the Pharos, let alone build one from raw materials. I can't even see the damage well enough to suggest possible repairs." His voice sank despairingly. "I never should have accepted this commission. I was lying to myself—right from the beginning."

"It isn't your fault," she cried, hating to hear his self-condemnation. "You didn't realize that Thomas was going to be left behind."

"And if Thomas were here, I might have used

his eyes somewhat—but not in a situation like this." The savagery in his voice stunned her. "Thomas is a competent draftsman, child, and may one day make a decent journeyman engineer, but if he had it in him to perform at this level he would already be out working on his own. No, a commission such as this requires a true engineer—one with keen vision."

"But you have the vision you need, Papa," she said, clinging to him, half crying herself. "Cassandra said so, remember? It was you that she and Edmund wanted to rebuild the Pharos. They could have gone anywhere in England— anywhere in the world—but the *Basset* sailed to Aldestow for *you!*"

"Oh, Emmie . . ." Defeated, James Alexander bent his head. "My dear, I do wish that that were so."

Footsteps tramped across the deck of the *Basset* over their heads. *I can't bear to see him like this,* Emily thought, biting back sobs. Tears wouldn't help her father. She had to convince him to believe in himself, but how? Then it hit her. *Cassandra—the <u>Basset</u>—the banner!*

"It *is* so!" she blurted out, pressing his hand more tightly. She prayed that she was right, that at last she understood what Cassandra had meant that day in the front hall at Petherick Place. It seemed so long ago. . . . "The *Basset*'s banner—it says *Credendo vides.* 'By believing, one sees.' If you believe, then you will be able to see—not with your eyes, but with your mind."

"But, child, a sighted man—"

"A sighted man! Thomas has eyes, but he can't see," she said scornfully. "You just said as much. It's your *vision* that's needed, Papa, not your eyes! Just like Cassandra said."

Vision. Such a simple word, but meaning so many things . . . a vision to believe in. "By believing, one sees." How simple could it be? So simple she hadn't understood. Emily held her breath, watching her father's face.

"I don't know," he said at last, slowly. "It doesn't seem . . ."

"Archimedes has faith in you, Papa," she said urgently. James Alexander respected the helmsman's judgment; he'd said so more than once on the voyage. "He told me he did."

"Archimedes believes in me?" Her father's blind eyes widened, obviously facing a brand-new idea.

"Yes, he does," she said, nodding in affirmation, though she knew he couldn't see the gesture. "And *I* believe in you, Papa. I—I might have doubted, sometimes . . . but I *do* believe."

And for the first time since the accident, it was absolutely true.

"Oh, Emmie, my dear . . ." Leaning forward,

he pulled her into his arms, embracing her. "My little girl. Just like your mother—Marian always believed in me, too. I think—I think, for a moment, I forgot that. . . ."

Fiercely, she hugged him back. "Well, now you remember. And you won't ever forget again. Will you?"

"No." Taking a deep breath, he straightened. "Which means that I—that we have a mirror to repair. I suppose we could try reinforcing that largest fragment. Although it would be better if . . ." He paused, blind eyes widening in sudden surprise. Emily could almost *see* the thought taking shape in his mind. She held her breath, waiting for it. "I hadn't—has Archimedes considered trying to use *all* of the largest Mirror fragments in some fashion?"

"You mean fitting them back together somehow?" Delighted, she scrambled to her feet. *This* was her father, back to life again. "I don't think so, but I haven't really talked to him since he and Captain Malachi returned to the ship."

"No, not fitting them together. But if there are at least three of any substance—and I believe there are at least three pieces large enough— then we *might* be able to contrive something in the French manner. Perhaps." Energetically, James Alexander stood, groping for his cane— but it was not a gesture of defeat or surrender this time. Emily found the cane leaning against the desk and thrust it into his hand. "Thank you, my dear." In the act of opening the cabin door, he stopped. "Thank you."

"You're welcome, Papa," Emily said, her heart overflowing. *Cassandra said he would need me. . . . Is this what she meant?* "I love you."

He touched her hair gently with one hand. "I know, Emmie. I love you, too."

On the deck of the *Basset,* everything was shrouded in gloom. Gremlins perched glumly on the railing, not even bothering to overset the bucket of sudsy water Seaman Augustus was using to mop the deck. Archimedes was polishing the *wuntarlabe*—preparing for departure? it seemed so—while Captain Malachi stood watching, his expression somber. Lewis was hovering nearby, too, evidently trying to be part of the railing. His arms were folded across his chest and he looked—stoic. Emily ignored him.

"Captain Malachi!" she called, guiding her father across the deck with a firm tug. "Papa has an idea. . . ."

"Have you, Mr. Engineer?" The captain brightened immediately. "I thought—but there, Archimedes *said* you would think of something if we just gave you enough time. What is it?"

"Yes. Well. It's only a possibility. . . ." James Alexander squared his shoulders. "Archimedes?"

"Yes, sir!" The helmsman beamed.

"What are the dimensions of the three largest fragments?"

"I have the figures here, sir." The dwarf pulled pages of notes from his pockets and scattered them across the deck in his eagerness; gremlins leaped to pick them up and hand them back to him before they blew into the water. "The largest one—"

"Never mind the largest one," James Alexander said firmly. The dwarf's face fell, but Emily's father plowed on. "What I have in mind is something quite different. If we build a carousel—a rotating carriage or cradle—we might be able to turn the pieces in a circle so that each reflects light into the other two in turn. The three together might then provide the necessary illumination—depending upon their relative size and shape, of course."

"A light that moves?" Captain Malachi sounded dubious. "I've never heard of such a thing."

Neither had Emily, but then, she wasn't a lighthouse engineer.

"It's a French innovation," James Alexander told them both—and an eager Archimedes, too. "The greater Fresnel lenses have to rotate in order to flash, and they are almost as massive as the Mirror—was. We may even be able to use some of the smaller fragments as refractors to increase the illumination. The trick will be to find a stable rotating mechanism, perhaps one that operates by clockwork."

"Like a grandfather clock?" Archimedes said, a frown creasing his forehead. "With gears, and a pendulum hanging down?"

"Not quite, but similar," Mr. Alexander said. He took a deep breath. "I can—I will describe the mechanism to you so that you can build it."

Emily watched, tears—happy tears this time—blurring her eyes again. Papa sounded so determined, so alive. So much like she remembered him from the years before the accident. Before Mama's death. She'd never dreamed . . .

Perhaps it was because she was watching and not really listening that she was the first to notice Lewis. The aggravating boy had taken no part in the conversation—hadn't even been paying attention, so far as Emily could tell. He'd just been standing in the prow of the ship, leaning against the rail and looking off into the distance—at the tower, she thought, though she couldn't be sure. Concerned, she moved closer. *What does he see out there?*

Suddenly, he stood up straight and walked over to where the *wuntarlabe* sat quietly humming on deck. Its wheels and gears and arrows were silent, but it glittered brilliantly even in the gray twilight.

Now what was the boy up to? Emily circled the deck, trying to get closer so she could keep an eye on him. His broad, stolid face was closed and blank, but there was something going on in that thick head, she was sure of it.

"We've equipment in the hold, of course," Captain Malachi was saying worriedly. "Cables and so on, for the rigging. I don't know if we've enough of what you'll be needing, though, Mr. Engineer. I don't know if I even know the *sort* of thing you'll be needing, exactly. I can't quite seem to see it, if you know what I mean. . . ."

"All we really require to begin is a wheel and a gearshaft," James Alexander assured him. "Although—given the immense height of the tower, the rotating base for the Mirror fragments will have to be *extremely* stable."

"Well, what about this thing?" Lewis asked suddenly, startling everyone. Two of the gremlins bounced off the rigging and went to stand beside him, looking curiously at where he was pointing, while Archimedes and the *Basset's* captain—and the lighthouse engineer—turned toward him in surprise.

"What do you mean, lad?" Captain Malachi said, speaking—Emily was sure—for all three.

"This." Lewis pointed at the *wuntarlabe* again, its gemmed central wheel turning idly as the *Basset* pulled at her mooring. "It's got a wheel, and it's big. Powerful, too, the way it turns about and about, no matter the tides. Can this *wuntar— wuntar*-whatsit—"

Emily's jaw dropped as she suddenly understood what he was getting at. What he meant. Lewis, of *all* people.

"*Wuntarlabe,*" Archimedes supplied, looking as astonished as Emily felt. "It's called a *wuntarlabe.*"

"Yeah, that. Whatever." Lewis hunched his shoulders. Off to one side, Sebastian beamed at him proudly. "I just thought—can this thing work on land?"

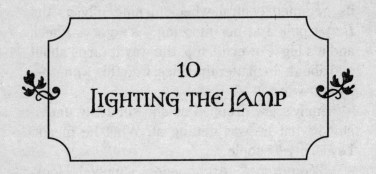

10
LIGHTING THE LAMP

Lewis had surprised Emily Alexander; he could tell by the stunned expression on her face. Privately, he admitted that he was pretty surprised himself. He'd just—*seen* the whole device, like a picture in his head, when Emily's father had started talking about rotating the Mirror remnants. If the *wuntarlabe* could open up and turn horizontally, so that its big central wheel was parallel to the ground, with the three largest pieces of the Mirror bolted onto the rim and spinning in a circle. . . . The whole thing seemed so obvious that he had a hard time understanding why no one else had thought of it first.

Emily Alexander seemed to agree with him about *that,* at least.

"Why?" she asked bluntly, coming up to him while Archimedes and a horde of excited gremlins swarmed over the *wuntarlabe*. "Why did you say it?"

"Because it'll work," he said, shying away slightly. The last time she'd spoken to him, she'd threatened to black his eye again, and he preferred not to take any chances. "See? The gremlins think so, too."

That seemed safe enough. The *Basset*'s shortest crew members were almost bouncing with exuberant approval.

"No, I meant why did you try to help at all?" she said, glowering. She was genuinely puzzled, he saw—and by her expression, she didn't like the feeling. "Even if you understood what Papa was talking about when no one else did—you *hate* lighthouses."

"No. I dun't," he said, not meeting her eyes. "I thought I did, but . . ." *I dun't hate the light.* That was one thing he was very sure of after being trapped in the darkness of the Basilisk's cave and facing the delighted maliciousness of the salamanders.

They're like my cousins, only worse, he thought, looking away from her. *Zach an' the others, they're just bullies. The salamanders, the Basilisk—they're* happy *when folks are hurt. If not liking lighthouses means being like that, then— well, I'm not, that's all. Dad will just have to understand.*

Aloud, he added: "Yer dad would have figured out the same thing, sooner or later."

"Maybe." She didn't sound convinced.

"It *will* work," James Alexander said exultantly, drawing all eyes back to him. He was on his knees on the deck of the *Basset,* examining the *wuntarlabe* with his hands. "If the gears are strong enough . . . Archimedes?"

"They *should* be strong enough," the helmsman said uncertainly. "Mind you, I don't know if anyone has ever considered using a *wuntarlabe* in such a fashion before. . . . Captain Malachi?"

"Not that I've heard," the captain said, scratching his beard. "I wish we had time to consult with the College of Magical Knowledge. But we haven't, so what's the point of wishing? Mr. Engineer, you see what others don't. If you truly *believe* that this will work . . ."

"I do," Mr. Alexander said at last, leaning back on his heels. "I truly do. But it will take some contriving."

"Then that's enough for me," Captain Malachi said decisively. "We'll try it. Well done, young Lewis."

"Aye, well done," echoed Sebastian, beaming fondly. The gremlins clapped their hats back on their heads and jumped up and down, tiny cheers ringing out.

Lewis could feel his face heating. *Blushing like a girl,* he thought, embarrassed. *What's come over me?*

Fortunately, he didn't have time to worry about it: there was too much work to do. First, they had to take apart the *wuntarlabe,* unbolt it from the deck, and carry it to the tower. The gremlins were responsible for that part, under the direction of Archimedes. Lewis helped as much as he could, mostly by acting as Mr. Alexander's eyes.

"We'll need precise measurements of every segment of the Mirror and of the *wuntarlabe*'s wheel," James Alexander warned him. "That way, we'll be able to draw the design of the mounting exactly to scale. Or rather, *you* will, at my direction."

Immediately, one of the gremlins pulled a sketch pad and a sharpened pencil out of his hat and offered them with a helpful bow. Lewis accepted the objects doubtfully. *Me? Draw to scale? What does that mean?* He'd never drawn much of anything before, but he supposed he could try.

"Yes, sir," he said, swallowing. "Draw to scale. Right."

The blind man's sharp ears picked up the boy's doubt. "Scale drawing is important, boy," he said, amusement lighting the lean, scarred face. "A good engineer has to calculate proportions before beginning to build, but he can't possibly design plans at life-size. What's the diameter of the wheel?"

"Uh . . ." Lewis still hadn't a clue what he was talking about. "I dun't—I'm not—"

"Well, we'll have to measure the straight line across the middle of the circle, in any case," James Alexander went on, a grin twitching at the corners of his mouth. Lewis didn't care; gratefully, he seized on the explanation in the blind man's words. So that was what a diameter was, was it? The line across the middle of a circle. He tucked the word into his memory for future reference. "Approximations have no place in engineering. An inch-to-a-foot scale will give us the initial design. If the wheel is four feet across, then you'll draw the circle representing the wheel with a diameter of four inches. If it's four feet, six inches, you will set the diameter at four and one-half inches."

"I get it!" Amazed, he realized that he did. "And if the biggest fragment is—is five feet tall at the tallest part, we'll draw it at five inches an' put it right where it's supposed to be on the wheel to catch the sun. And so on!"

"Exactly." Mr. Alexander sounded pleased. "The difficult part will be positioning each fragment so that it both reflects light from the other two pieces and emits a beam from its own central point. . . . That will require careful calculation."

"We can do it," Lewis said sturdily, looking at Emily's father with new respect. *Imagine being able to figure things like that in yer head.* . . . "You tell me how, an' I'll draw all you want."

He'd said something like that to the Basilisk once, he remembered guiltily—but this time, he meant it with his whole heart.

The *wuntarlabe* was only part of the work, of course—there was also the Mirror to be prepared. Lewis didn't have much to do with that, fortunately—he scarcely had time to sleep, as it was!—but when he had the chance, he watched respectfully as Emily and Sebastian polished the fragments and smoothed the jagged edges of each broken piece. It was painstaking, tedious work, possible only in daylight, when the fragments didn't burn whatever touched them. Emily and Sebastian worked carefully, using soft chamois and silk for a final burnishing.

"We're almost finished," she reported on the afternoon of the fifth day after the Basilisk's attack. "Sebastian is just smoothing out the edges on the last piece. He wants to know if we should carry the fragments up to the tower yet."

Two days until the solstice, by Lewis's

calculations. One until Midsummer's Eve. He still wasn't quite sure why the summer solstice was their deadline, but he'd decided that it didn't matter. Emily's father said it was, and so did Captain Malachi and Archimedes and Sebastian. That was enough for him.

"Yes—yes, we should," James Alexander said now, absently wiping his hands on a bit of cloth. He'd been fingering the spare gears from the *wuntarlabe,* trying to decide how they should be placed. "Is the wheel ready?"

"All set, Mr. Engineer," Archimedes said, saluting smartly. "On top of the tower, just as you commanded."

It had been decided to fix the Mirror fragments onto the *wuntarlabe* for the first time once the device was already in place, rather than trying to assemble the device on the ground and carry it up. As it was, it took three dwarves and Lewis the rest of the day to get the three pieces up the stairs, and when they finally set the last one down on the platform, Lewis felt as though he'd been climbing mountains. In a way, he had been.

Working together, he and Archimedes lifted each polished piece of the Mirror and fitted it into the niche prepared for it, while James Alexander and Emily waited. She was holding

her father's hand, as usual, while Captain
Malachi and the rest of the crew stood around
the edge of the platform.

"There, that's done it," Archimedes grunted,
locking the last fragment into place. "Pretty as a
picture, isn't it."

They stepped back a moment to admire their
handiwork: the three Mirror fragments, perfectly
balanced on the wheel of the *wuntarlabe* and sitting in the mathematically exact center of the
tower.

Captain Malachi nodded. "That it is, Helmsman. That it is." Taking out a gold pocket watch,
he checked the time. "Tomorrow at sunset, then,
Mr. Engineer?"

"Tomorrow at sunset, Captain," Emily's
father said, his voice firm.

Lewis couldn't sleep that night. Shut up in his
small cabin on the *Basset,* he listened to the slap
of the waves and the creak of the ship's mast and
tried to count sheep, but it was no use. What if it
didn't work? They'd bet everything on this one
try. It ought to work, Mr. Alexander said, and he
should know, but if it *didn't* . . . then what?

Nothing, that's what, he thought, tossing rest-
lessly in his bunk. *We go home an' the tower stays
dark for another five hundred years.*

He didn't like the thought of that, after all of

their hard work. At least Captain Malachi had posted a proper night guard on the platform. It would have been better if they could have sealed the door to the Basilisk's tunnel again, but Sebastian said that wasn't possible: once the door had been opened, it was open, and they would just have to live with the consequences.

Lewis didn't like the thought of *that,* either, but there was nothing he could do about it now—about any of it. When he finally dozed off, he dreamed he was being chased down the wharf at Aldestow by hissing salamanders, while his cousins stood by and jeered.

Next evening. Sunset. The benu swooped in and out of the pillars on the platform, sparks lighting the shadows.

"They know something's up," Lewis said, watching them.

"Well, of course." Sebastian smiled at him. They were all crowded together on top of the tower for the ceremony, all except Bosun Eli, who had been left on watch. "It is their ancient charge, to protect the Mirror."

"Until I came along," Lewis said, looking away. He'd avoided the benu as much as he could since that horrible night when the Mirror fell. They'd tried to warn him, and he hadn't listened.

"Now, lad, I didn't mean—"

"Very well." James Alexander stood up from his last inspection of the Mirror's *wuntarlabe*-based mounting and moved away. "It's as sturdy as we can make it. Helmsman Archimedes, I believe this is your department. . . ."

"Eh? Oh—yes, sir! Aye, aye, sir!" Pulling a scrap of paper from his waistcoat pocket, the dwarf bent and began to turn knobs and pull levers to set the *wuntarlabe*. He had to reach rather far around for some of them, and at one point actually lay full-length on the floor to twiddle with a hidden gear—but at last, the *wuntarlabe* was set. "All done, sir."

Lewis held his breath. A dwarf to set the *wuntarlabe* and a gremlin to spin it, that was what Captain Malachi had told them. If the newly mounted Mirror was going to work, then this would be the moment. *If*. The tallest gremlin of the crew stepped forward, took off his even taller hat, and bowed several times ceremoniously in a circle. Then he clapped his hat back on his head, stuck the tip of his littlest finger into an opening on the horizontal *wuntarlabe,* and wiggled it.

Slowly, slowly, gears began to move. The Mirror quivered ever so slightly. Emily gasped. "It's moving! Papa, the wheel is turning!"

"Downstairs, everyone," Malachi said, urgently shooing them off the platform. "Quickly!

We don't want to be up here when the Mirror starts to burn. Besides, we'll see better from outside."

Down the long spiral staircase they went, half in shadow, with gremlins scampering and skittering back and forth on every step and the sparks of excited benu birds lighting their way. Out into the clearing in front of the tower, where the broken Mirror had rested—until Captain Malachi held up a hand. "Far enough," he said.

"Now what?" Lewis asked, panting slightly.

"Now we wait, boy," James Alexander said tautly, his scarred face pale in the twilight. He reached out to place one hand on Lewis's shoulder and took his daughter's arm with the other; she nodded at Lewis, accepting his presence. Somehow, it felt right to Lewis, the three of them standing together like that. "We wait and watch."

"Look up!" Archimedes said, pointing. "Look, look up at the tower!"

There wasn't a sound on the whole island; even the benu were quiet, waiting.

The glow was dim at first, a soft, muffled halo that might have been moonlight shining through water. Or a distant hearth fire, seen from a hillside far away. . . . slowly, slowly, unthinkably gradually, the light gathered strength, gathered force—began to shine with the brilliance of a captured star. Lewis caught his breath, hoping against hope—praying. *Let it be bright enough. Oh, Saint Piran, let it work. . . .*

And then, suddenly, almost too suddenly to see, a great beam of rosy gold light bloomed from the tower platform, flaring out into the night sky. Gremlins leapt up and down, cheering lustily, while benu birds took flight in a squawking, showering spiral of delight.

"We've done it!" Captain Malachi roared, both arms shooting into the air in triumph. He grabbed Archimedes and swung him around in an impromptu jig of celebration. "The Pharos is restored!"

The crew clapped hands, shouted, "Hurrah!" and joyously threw hats in the air. To Lewis's utter shock, Emily flung her arms around him and kissed his cheek.

"Hey, watch it!" Lewis protested, trying to get a hand free to wipe the kiss off. *She didn't have to do that.* But he found himself grinning foolishly right back at her.

"It's lit!" she cried exuberantly. "It's beautiful!"

It was beautiful, the most beautiful thing he'd ever seen. But Emily's father was just standing there in the middle of all the noise, head tilted back to look upward as if he could see for himself—and suddenly Lewis was furious that he *couldn't* see. The Maker of Lights, the Basilisk had called James Alexander. It didn't seem fair that he should make light for others to see by, yet have none for himself. . . .

Then, while they were still celebrating, another light twinkled into being under the palm trees—a smaller one, not nearly so bright. Instantly, Lewis tensed, wondering if somehow the Basilisk—but Captain Malachi went to greet the newcomers almost as if he'd been expecting them.

"Welcome, King Oberon, Queen Titania," he said, bowing. "Welcome to the Lighthouse at Pharos."

"Well met, good Malachi," the king— Oberon?—said, smiling. He was tall and white-haired, and wore a simple golden crown on his head. Beside him walked a woman in a gossamer gown of white. Lewis had never heard of a king named Oberon or a queen named Titania, but he had no doubt that these were very important people. Emily's eyes were round with awe. "You and your crew have done nobly in the task that was assigned to you."

"Well met by starlight and by Mirror light," the queen said in a warm, gentle voice. "Our thanks."

Malachi blushed and mumbled something

into his beard. Lewis grinned.

"It was our engineer's doing, mostly," the *Basset*'s captain said, nodding bashfully at James Alexander. "We just helped. Mr. Alexander, it is my honor to present to you King Oberon and Queen Titania, king and queen of our Lands of Legend. Your Majesties, this is James Alexander, noted lighthouse engineer, his daughter, Miss Emily, and his assistant, Lewis Trelawny."

James bowed. Emily curtsied. Lewis didn't move. *Assistant? I'm no one's assistant. I'm just—*

Emily kicked him, catching him painfully in the shins. Hastily, he bowed, too.

"Our thanks, indeed, Mr. Engineer," Oberon said, glancing upward at the great light shining into the darkness. "You have given my lands a wonder."

"It is only fitting, Sire," James answered steadily, but Lewis could see his hands trembling. "The legend of the Pharos gave the idea of lighthouses to the world, once upon a time. All we have done here is return the favor."

"A bit more than that, I suspect," Queen Titania said, glancing mischievously at Lewis. "So, Lewis Trelawny, did you enjoy your long sea voyage?"

"What?" Lewis's mouth fell open. *How could she—she sounds like that Cassandra, the one with the necklace.* "Yes, I did," he said slowly, realizing that it was true. "Well, not the being seasick part, or the Basilisk. But everything else I enjoyed very much."

"The Basilisk?" Oberon frowned. "Has the Lord of the Little Darknesses been freed? To what purpose?"

Lewis wasn't quite sure how to answer that—though "Lord of the Little Darknesses" struck him as a very good name for the Basilisk. He opened his mouth to say as much and was interrupted by a noise from the harbor. The *Basset*'s alarm bell!

"Sir! Sir!" Bosun Eli rushed up in excitement, his mustache all askew. He had the spyglass in his outstretched hand. "See! He comes! He comes!"

"What? Where?" Snatching the glass, Malachi pointed it at the eastern sky. "Already? It isn't even full dark!"

"What is it?" James asked anxiously. "Emmie? Lewis? What are they talking about?"

"I—I don't . . ." Straining eastward, Lewis stood on tiptoe to see. "It's a bird! A bird of fire!"

Soaring over the edge of the horizon was a great bird, its tail flaming behind it. Light glowing around it as though it were a piece of the sun come to earth, it flew straight into the Mirror's beam, gilded even further by that incredible brilliance. Beautiful, powerful, strong, filling the sky

with fire . . . gliding effortlessly toward Pharos.
Lewis stared, transfixed.

"The Phoenix," Oberon breathed, head
thrown back to see and handsome face alight.
"The king of all birds returns at last to the Lands
of Legend. Oh, thank you, Mr. Engineer! Thank
you!"

"The Phoenix!" Mr. Alexander's voice was triumphant. "I knew it! Heliopolis, the city of the
sun, home of the legendary Phoenix—oh, daughter, children, tell me! Tell me what you see!"

"A bird of fire," Lewis repeated obediently,
frantically seeking words. How could he describe
something like this? Something he'd never even
imagined? "Its feathers're gold and red, and they
burn like—like a bonfire on Guy Fawkes, on'y
brighter. It soars with its wings spread out—"

"Like an eagle," Emily interrupted, her eyes
shining. "But bigger, Papa, much bigger! Its
wings must be ten, twelve feet across! They
shine even brighter than the stars. . . ."

"The benu birds are going crazy," Lewis said,
noticing for the first time that all of the fireworks
birds had taken wing. "They're flying up to meet
it—"

"Not just the benu," Emily corrected him, but
he didn't mind at all. "Other birds, too! They're
flying with the Phoenix. Listen to them!"

She was right. All birds that ever wore

feathers were soaring in the air above the island, circling and swooping and calling to each other. Little sparrows and red-tailed hawks, eagles and swallows and wrens, seagulls and bitterns and curlews and tiny hummingbirds—even crows and grackles spiraled around the Phoenix, weaving pattern after triumphant pattern across the horizon. The purple wings of the benu flashed with light, echoing their flight. The sky was as bright as day. Emily was crying openly now, clutching at her father's hand. Lewis didn't blame her. He wanted to cry and clutch, too. It was too much beauty, too much power—too magnificent for words to speak or eyes to see. . . .

One by one, the great feathered ranks settled, filling the ground and the palm trees and clinging to the stones of the tower. Alone, the Phoenix circled the Mirror once, twice, three times, as if paying homage. Then, as softly as a falling leaf, it landed in front of them.

Oberon bowed. "Greetings, Lord of Birds," the king said, his voice dark with emotion. Beside him, Titania offered a queenly curtsy of her own. "Welcome home."

"Greetings, Lord and Lady of Legends," the Phoenix said, its voice chiming like all music. James Alexander leaned forward, as if hearing in those golden tones the beauty all the rest of them saw, Lewis thought, blinking back a suspicious mistiness. "It has been too long since the Light burned for my return."

"And would have been longer, were it not for this human and his companions." Stepping back, Oberon gestured at James.

"A mortal?" The golden, glowing eyes turned toward Emily's father, surprised. "A mortal has been the vessel of my return?"

"A lighthouse engineer, Lord of Birds," Oberon corrected, smiling ever so slightly. "One who builds lighthouses in the lands of mortals, to guide them through the darkness of the endless night."

"So . . ." The feathered head bent so that that powerful beak was just a little too close to James Alexander for Lewis's liking. Gulping, he stepped up beside Emily's father, hands clenching into fists. But the Phoenix's next words weren't hostile. "I owe my return to a man of science," it said, bemused. "Marvelous, indeed."

"No one said that a man of science cannot also be a man of belief, King of Birds," James Alexander said boldly, standing tall. Lewis wanted to cheer again, just for him. "My daughter and my assistant know that well. In some ways, they have taught me."

"Well said, Engineer," the Phoenix answered,

its beak opening in what had to be a smile. "My gratitude to you, then, and to your daughter and your assistant—"

"The traitor!" A raucous, screeching voice from the shadows under the trees. A slithering, strutting movement forward—and Lewis shrank back, suddenly terrified out of his wits. The Basilisk! *No. Not now!* It couldn't be . . . but it was. "The boy is *Ours,* King of Birds! We claim him, by the writ and the rule of ancient law. He is Ours, as are all traitors!"

11
The Trial

Emily couldn't believe it. After everything that had happened . . . First the Mirror was broken and all was lost; then the Mirror was mended and they had a chance. Now, just as they'd won—as the lamp was lit, and the Phoenix returned—how *dare* this hideous monster come along to ruin everything? She wanted to scream at the very idea.

But the Phoenix didn't seem the least bit disturbed, or even surprised, by the interruption. Regally calm, it did no more than lift its magnificent wings slightly, as if in welcome. Around it, benu birds sparked indignantly, but it quieted them with a look.

"Greetings, darker brother," it said to the Basilisk, beautiful voice chiming musically. "What is it that you wish?"

His brother! Oh, I don't like the sound of that!
One so dark and misshapen and ugly, the other
so golden and marvelous ... Emily glanced from
one to the other, comparing. *They don't look a
thing alike.*

"Greetings, royal bird," the Basilisk said with
a sneer. "We wish Our own again. This boy"—a
stubby wing pointed directly at Lewis—"this boy
promised Us his allegiance and then betrayed
Us. We say again, the traitor is *Ours!*"

Around the Basilisk and behind it, salamanders lifted arrow-shaped heads to bare vicious
teeth. Lewis took a half step backward, going
gray as ashes.

"What does he mean?" Emily whispered to
him behind her hand. *Lewis was captured by those
things? Oh, poor Lewis.* For the first time, she felt
a real stirring of sympathy for the Aldestow boy.
No wonder he looks so dreadful. "How did you
betray him?"

"I promised to help him an' the salamanders
break the Mirror," he said, low-voiced. "An' then
I tried to stop them."

"Well, but you shouldn't have promised in the
first place—"

"We must have a trial," the Phoenix announced. Oberon looked concerned but
nodded slowly. Titania clasped her hands before
her and looked away. "Will that content

you, darker brother?" the Phoenix asked.

"A trial ... ye-es." The Basilisk bent its rooster head to glare at Lewis. "A trial that We will win."

"That remains to be seen," the Phoenix said remotely. "Lord of Legends? How much time will you need to prepare?"

"No time! No time!" the Basilisk squawked, flapping its stubby wings. "The traitor stands accused! Let him be tried and condemned at once!"

"Silence!" the Phoenix's golden voice thundered. Like a pricked balloon, the scaly monster subsided, but it still jittered back and forth on its toes, for all the world like a rooster waiting to crow. "Fairy King?"

"An hour, King of Birds," Oberon said, bowing slightly. "No more than an hour."

Oberon, it appeared, was to be counsel for the defense. He at once took Lewis off to the side to question him privately about his testimony.

"He knows humans best of all of us, you see," Sebastian explained when Emily asked him why.

"But he's king," she objected. "Can't he just— well—declare Lewis innocent?"

"Oh, no." Sebastian looked shocked. "Kings have to obey laws, too, or what's the use of having any?"

"Kings or laws?" she asked, confused.

"Why, both . . . or either." Sebastian sighed, shaking his head worriedly. "The Phoenix rules on Pharos, Miss Emily. He rules fairly, and with justice, but . . . if Lewis truly did promise to help the Basilisk, I fear it will go ill for him."

Oh, dear. Emily didn't like the sound of *that,* either. But surely the beautiful Phoenix couldn't be cruel? Covertly, she examined the splendid bird, waiting patiently by the base of the tower. Sebastian had told her that the Phoenix normally roosted on the platform where the Mirror was— it was why they hadn't put any roof on the top— but first he would clear up this business. *He does have a stern look about him.*

The *Basset* crew members ranged themselves to the left, subdued gremlins in front of worried dwarves. Clearly, they were on Lewis's side; equally clearly, they had no power to intervene. James Alexander hadn't said a word since the Basilisk had made its accusation. He'd just stood silently—listening, Emily thought. Oberon had kept his conversation with Lewis quiet, but she didn't think that the fairy king quite understood how keen her father's hearing was.

"We are ready, King of Birds," Oberon announced after what seemed like far too short a time.

At the fairy king's words, James Alexander shifted slightly and touched his daughter's arm.

"Stand with me, Emmie," he said slowly. "Behind Lewis. He shouldn't be alone."

No. No, he shouldn't be, she thought, moving obediently into place.

"You stand accused of treachery, mortal," the Phoenix said, every word falling into the silence like pearls into a dish. "Is this true?" Lewis hung his head, not answering. The Phoenix persisted. "Is this true?"

"I—yes, sir," the Cornish boy said finally, wretchedly. His voice cracked embarrassingly on the last word. "Yer Majesty. I promised I'd help him wreck the Mirror, and then I tried to stop it—to stop *them* from doing what they were doing." He nodded at the huddled salamanders. The Basilisk hissed in triumph, its cock's comb lifting. "King Oberon says I've got—got no choice but to throw myself upon the mercy o' the court."

"Mercy!" The Basilisk sneered malevolently. It slithered forward a few feet, rooster legs dangling. Lewis jerked backward but held his ground. "Such treachery merits no mercy. We proclaim it! The boy sought to assist where he had sworn to prevent—even to lighting the lamp that burns now on top of the tower. Ask him! Ask him and these others if it is not so!"

The Phoenix glanced around the clearing inquiringly. The *Basset* crew members looked down and away and scuffled their feet in the dirt; nervous gremlins removed their hats and then put them back on again, over and over. Emily bit her lip. Lewis *had* been the one to think of using the *wuntarlabe*.

"He's only a boy," James Alexander said, frowning. "Surely—"

"Age does not excuse treachery," the Basilisk interrupted, opening and closing its dangling claws. "Eh, bird brother?"

"It is so," the Phoenix said sadly.

"But, Lord of Birds, do not the errors of youth call for mercy?" Oberon asked softly. Emily wanted to applaud. About time counsel for the defense spoke up! "The boy has admitted his error and begged forgiveness. It is age and experience that bring wisdom. . . ."

"Forgiveness!" Throwing back its head, the Basilisk uttered a shrill cock's crow that made Emily's skin crawl. "We grant no forgiveness. Justice, We say. Vengeance is Ours!"

"But vengeance isn't justice," Oberon said, even more softly.

"No. It isn't," James Alexander said, taking a deep breath. He stepped forward. "King of Birds, excuse my impertinence, but I wonder—I am not aware of—that is, what is the customary penalty for treachery in the Lands of Legend?"

The Phoenix turned its beautiful head toward

him. "The traitor returns to the darkness, to the cave of the Basilisk, there to serve for the term of his life. As he refused service, so he must give it freely."

Emily was appalled. "You mean Lewis would have to live the rest of his life in a cave full of horrible *lizards*?"

Horrible hissing and laughter from the Basilisk—and from his salamanders, who seemed to find her exclamation very amusing.

"Where do you think Our salamanders came from, mortal child?" the rooster-turned-snake said, beak clacking. Its tail lashed out, bowling over the salamanders clustered around it. "Treachery was ever a human thing. Is this not fair? Is it not *justice*?"

"But—but—" Sickened, she stared at the salamanders, who cringed from her as if in shame. The lizards—transformed humans? It couldn't be. And yet, they *were* roughly human-shaped, when she looked at them. They all had four limbs, if rather deformed. Smallish, crouched-over humans—*boy-sized* humans, some of them, covered in scales—might well come to look something like that. The very idea made her want to vomit. And Lewis looked worse than he had when he was seasick. He swayed as if he were going to faint. "No! You can't do that to Lewis! He's only a boy!"

At the same instant, her father said, "Lord Basilisk—"

"King Basilisk!" the monster shrilled instantly. "We are King!"

"I cry pardon." The engineer inclined his head. "King Basilisk, then. I am responsible for this boy's presence on Pharos, and for his actions, good or ill. That being the case, I believe that a substitution might be made—might it not?"

"What do you propose?" the Basilisk said, intrigued. Its comb lifted and then lay flat.

"I propose that I come to your cave, and live with you and serve you, in place of Lewis," James Alexander said resolutely.

"Indeed." The Basilisk slithered closer to him, forked tongue flickering. The salamanders stirred uneasily. "A Maker of Lights, in my service. It requires thought."

Not to Emily, it didn't. Her father—turned into a lizard? She gasped in raw horror. *"No!"*

"Have you given good thought to this, Engineer?" Oberon said, troubled. "To live forever in darkness . . ."

"You forget my lack of sight, Sire," James said, shrugging self-deprecatingly. He seemed quite calm, but Emily could tell he wasn't. His arm was shaking badly beneath her hand. "I daresay I won't even miss the light—all that much. So long as Captain Malachi and the *Basset* are able to see Emily and Lewis safely home . . ."

"I'm not going without you," Emily said, clutching at him in terror.

"Me either," Lewis said, inelegantly but truculently. He wasn't swaying anymore. Instead, he looked—determined. "Mr. Alexander, sir, you can't. It's you the Basilisk has wanted all along. You were the one he was really trying to kill when he turned the Mirror on the *Basset*. You can't let him win like that."

"Lad, you're too young to know what you're saying—"

"No, I'm not," Lewis said stubbornly. "If anyone goes into that cave, or—or gets turned into a lizard—it's goin' to be me, and that's final. I'm the one who broke my promise, an' I'm the one who should pay. It's on'y fair."

"No, Lewis! Don't say that!" Emily cried. If it came to a choice between her father and Lewis . . . but she didn't want *anyone* to have to go with the Basilisk. *I couldn't bear it.* "It isn't fair! You didn't mean—"

Understanding struck her with such force that she almost gasped, and had to grab her father's arm to keep from falling over.

"It dun't matter what I meant or didn't mean," Lewis argued, looking away. Looking ill. "I did it. . . ."

"It does too matter!" Emily said, turning

eagerly to the Phoenix. "Sir—Lord of Birds—the Basilisk *lied* to Lewis. Yes, and he lied again here, tonight! He asked Lewis to promise to help break the Mirror, all right, but he didn't say that he was going to use the Mirror to burn the *Basset*! *That* was when Lewis turned against him. Not before!"

Oberon's head lifted alertly. "If that is true— Lewis?"

"Yeah. It's true." The Aldestow boy sounded confused. "I guess. But what difference does it—"

"It would make a difference at home," James Alexander said, scarred face taking on an intent, hopeful expression. "In England, a contract entered into under false pretenses constitutes fraud, and the defrauded party is not obligated to fulfill it."

How did Papa know—oh, of course. Emily felt a surge of pride. Her father had signed *many* contracts during his days as a working engineer, and he'd always done his best to live up to them.

"And in the Lands of Legend as well, I believe," Oberon said joyously. He stepped forward and bowed to the Phoenix. "King of Birds, as counsel for the defense, I move that we dismiss all charges—"

"No!" The Basilisk beat the air, outraged. "A vow is a vow. We will have vengeance!"

"Vengeance is not justice, my darker

brother," the Phoenix reminded it. "You stand accused of fraud—and of bearing false witness in your accusation against this boy. Does the mortal child speak truth?"

The snake's tail coiled and uncoiled. "Well— ah—that is, I . . ."

It forgot to say "We," Emily noticed gleefully.

"Answer!" Music became thunder in a single word. *"Is—this—true?"*

"Yes!" the Basilisk shrieked, flapping its stubby wings in panic. "Light burn you—darkness take you—yes!"

Around it, salamanders wailed in hissing panic, fleeing back under the trees. Emily clapped her hands in delight.

"They're leaving! They're all—Lewis, you're safe! We're all safe!"

He just *looked* at her with his mouth open, as if he couldn't understand a word she was saying.

"Didn't you hear me? I said—"

But the Phoenix wasn't finished. Spreading burning wings before the cowering Basilisk, it spoke in a voice *beyond* thunder.

"I banish you, my darker brother," it said. Light dripped from the long primary feathers, igniting the very air. "Go! By the writ and the rule that you yourself have invoked, by the ancient law that you obey and I impose, get you back to the dark places from whence you came, and trouble the daylight no more!"

The Basilisk screamed, a high, thin noise. Brighter and brighter the Phoenix glowed, the sun come down to earth. How had the tower burned? All at once, Emily thought she knew the answer to that question. She tried to watch, tears streaming out of her eyes. Off to one side, she caught a glimpse of Lewis, hands plastered over his face. Archimedes and Sebastian were clinging to each other, with Captain Malachi bent almost double in front of them. The king and queen of fairies alone stood upright, facing the shining beauty of the Phoenix with awe on both their faces.

And then the flames were too bright, too hot, for any gaze to bear. Emily had to bend her own head against them, eyes tightly shut, taking shelter in her father's arms. . . .

Slowly, slowly, the light and the flames died away. When Emily dared to open her eyes again, the first thing she saw was the Phoenix, its fires dimmed to bearable levels. Above, the beam of the Mirror still cast its own steady light into the night sky, exactly as her father and Archimedes—and Lewis—had decreed: a light against the darkness.

Lewis smiled at her tremulously, walking over to join her on legs that seemed more than a little shaky. She smiled back, equally tremulous, as her father helped her to stand. The Aldestow boy held out his hand in front of his face, looking at it as if he couldn't quite believe that the ordeal was over and he was still himself. Still there. But he was. They all were.

Only the Basilisk and its salamanders were gone.

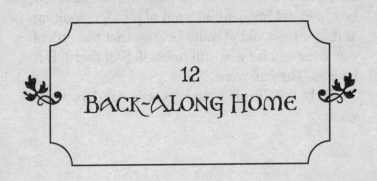

12
BACK-ALONG HOME

Going back-along home, Lewis thought content-edly, leaning both elbows on the *Basset's* railing and watching while chortling gremlins chased sparking benu birds through the shallow waters by the shore. It was late afternoon at Pharos, and the sun was comfortably warm on his shoulders. *About time, too.*

He no longer doubted that he'd be in Aldestow almost before his mother had had a chance to miss him—or that, if she had, Cassandra would have reassured her. The *Basset* was magical enough that anything was possible, even a journey of weeks that seemed to take no more than a few hours. Sebastian didn't even think Lewis would be seasick on the return voyage.

"You don't feel out of place on the *Basset* anymore, lad," the elderly dwarf had said, patting his shoulder. "You've earned your passage."

Lewis wasn't so sure, but—well, he'd have to risk it. It was time to go home.

A magnificent splash caught his attention, and he grinned. One of the benu had grabbed a gremlin's hat in its long beak and run away with it, stilt-like legs churning water. The gremlin raced after it, howling insults. Of course, the bird could have escaped with its booty merely by flying, but that, it appeared, would have been against the rules. And both sides apparently enjoyed the game too much to wish to bring it to an end.

Rules . . . Lewis's grin faded as he realized just how close he'd come to disaster by breaking a rule he hadn't known existed. If it hadn't been for Emily and her father, he might even now be trapped in a dark cave, growing scales and claws, instead of . . . he shivered.

Dad got sent to Australia for breaking the law when he didn't mean to, he thought. *He didn't have anyone like Emily to speak up for him, or anyone to stand with him, like Mr. Alexander stood with me. . . . I got off easy.*

Easy in more ways than one, which was another reason he was glad to be leaving the island. The Basilisk had been banished, but not forever. Oberon had been very clear about that.

"One day, the door to its cave will no doubt be

opened again," the king had said almost apologetically to James Alexander, watching while Archimedes and the gremlins dismantled the light. The *Basset* needed the *wuntarlabe* for the return voyage—and with the Phoenix in residence, the tower had more than enough light to guide any straying mariners. "The power of the dark must be acknowledged, even in the Lands of Legend."

"Of course." The engineer nodded, his sightless eyes turning outward toward where the Phoenix roosted in glory. "How could we value the light without some darkness for it to shine in?"

A blind man saying something like that, and meaning it . . . Remembering, Lewis shook his head. Captain Malachi had been right: Emily's father *could* see what others didn't, even without his eyes.

Even more astonishing was what the engineer had said to Lewis that very morning. They'd been standing together companionably on the deck of the *Basset,* almost where Lewis was standing now. No one else was around, not even Emily. Lewis had haltingly expressed his gratitude, and James Alexander had waved it away—not dismissively, as unimportant, but as something that didn't need to be discussed further.

"You wouldn't have been in danger if you hadn't tried to protect me—and my daughter and the crew of the *Basset*—from being burned to death," the blind man reminded him. "Let's not forget that. Now. Have you given any thought to your plans when we return to Aldestow?"

Lewis blinked, puzzled by the change of subject. "See my mum, I guess—find out if Uncle Jos is really mad . . ."

"He won't be," James Alexander predicted confidently. "Or if he is, come to me. I may not be an expert at dealing with basilisks or salamanders, but I can handle Josiah Trelawny well enough."

"You—you know my uncle?" Lewis asked cautiously.

"Yes." He smiled, reminiscing, the scarred face surprisingly boyish. "We were friends once, back when I was an apprentice engineer and had just met Emily's mother. . . . Never mind that now. What I meant was, have you given any thought to your future?"

James Alexander and Uncle Jos? *Friends?* The mind boggled. But—

"Not really," Lewis answered him, shrugging. "Go into the mines when I'm old enough, I suppose, since Mum's so dead against the sea. Well, not the sea, 'zactly, but wrecking. Still . . ."

"The mines . . . hmm." Mr. Alexander was

apparently absorbed in the feel of the *Basset*'s railing beneath his hands. "A hard life, underground."

Lewis shrugged again. "Not much choice for an Aldestow wrecker's boy. Anyway, all I ever really wanted was to earn enough money so Mum and me could join Dad in Australia."

Not much chance of that, either, he thought, but without bitterness. Life in the tin mines might be dark and dangerous and filled with hard labor, but it was better than the cave of the Basilisk any day of the week and twice on Sundays.

"The thing is . . . ," said Mr. Alexander. Deep breath; Lewis had noticed that Emily's father always seemed to take a deep breath whenever he had something difficult to say. "The thing is, you have the makings of an engineer."

"What?" Wherever Lewis had expected this conversation to go, he certainly hadn't expected that. "An engineer? *Me?* Buildin' lighthouses an' all?"

"And bridges and dams," Mr. Alexander confirmed. "Engineers *see* things and then work to make them real. That's what you did in designing the mounting for the lamp out of the *Basset*'s *wuntarlabe.*"

"But—but—" Engineers were professional

men. For an Aldestow boy in his position even to dream of such a thing was—was unheard of. "I couldn't afford the schooling. Could I?"

"An engineering apprenticeship is expensive," Emily's father told him judiciously. "However, you might work your way through—room and board and education in exchange for, say, assisting your master in his own projects. Assuming that you had a master who required a certain amount of physical assistance, that is."

"You mean *you*?" Lewis blurted out. "I could—could learn from you, and live up at Petherick Place, in exchange for helping you draw and take notes like I did on the island?"

It was Mr. Alexander's turn to shrug. "It seems possible. My current apprentice is more of a secretary than an engineering student, really. I could use another—perhaps more than one."

"What about my mum? I dun't want her to have to stay at Uncle Josiah's. . . ."

"I'm sure something could be arranged," Emily's father said confidently. "Perhaps an assistant housekeeper's position, or—well, we can figure it out later."

Me. An engineer. The idea glittered as brightly as the Phoenix—and seemed just as impossible. But the Phoenix *was* real. Maybe—

maybe Engineer Lewis Trelawny could be a reality, too? If he believed in it . . .

"They need lighthouses in Australia, too, you know," Mr. Alexander said persuasively.

"They do?" Lewis had never thought of that.

"Yes, and dams, and bridges, and—oh, all sorts of things that a young engineer determined to make his way in the world might design and build. It's a whole new continent, after all, surrounded by ocean—think about it." He paused. "That's all I'm asking you to do, for now. Just—think about it."

"All right," Lewis said slowly. Cassandra had asked much the same thing, he remembered. *I will.* . . .

Hours later, he was still thinking about it, and still half afraid that if he thought too long, the whole bright dream might slip away. He'd have to ask Mum, of course—but there wasn't much doubt that *she'd* like the idea. A chance to live in the big house on the hill, and for her boy to go to school instead of going wrecking or into the mines? She'd be more than happy. Even if Mr. Alexander gave them two pokey rooms down in the cellar to live in, that would be better than what they had at Uncle Josiah's—probably less work, too. He looked out at the still-frolicking gremlins and benu birds without really seeing them. The only thing was . . .

"Hello." Emily Alexander, coming up behind him, took him completely by surprise. He shied away, and then caught himself when he realized who it was.

"Dun't sneak up on a person like that," he said, annoyed at his own nervousness. He still had occasional dreams of being chased by salamanders.

"Sorry." She didn't sound it. Well, maybe he was being too sensitive. "What's the matter? You aren't getting sick again, are you?"

"No." Sighing, he turned back to lean his elbows on the railing again. "I was just—just thinkin' about what yer dad said this morning."

"About you becoming his apprentice?" she asked acutely, leaning beside him. "You are going to, aren't you?"

"You—you dun't mind?" That was the thing that held him back: how Emily Alexander would react to her father's offer.

"Of course not," she said calmly. "Thomas is a complete waste as an engineer, even I can tell that. Papa says you're already a better apprentice just from working with him on the island. And it's a big house—too big for the two of us, really. There are rooms we never even open except to air them out."

"Well . . ." He knew it was a big house. *The* big house in Aldestow. That was the problem.

"I mean it," she insisted, sensing that he doubted her. "You and your mother could have rooms upstairs on the third floor so you would have some privacy. She could help with the cooking and the housekeeping—Mrs. Giffey only comes in days, and she's been wanting to go live with her married daughter over in Newquay, anyway—and you could work with Papa. It would be perfect."

"Got it all figured out, haven't you," he said, half admiringly, half resentfully. "What if I dun't want to?"

She sniffed. "You'd be a fool not to want to. If Papa says you have the talent to be an engineer, then you do. He's always been good at training apprentices. That's why—" She stopped suddenly, flushing, as if she'd said more than she should have.

"Why what?" Lewis asked, curious.

"Papa's been talking about starting a school." With the tip of her toe, she traced a pattern on the deck. "Just the past few days. He could do it, you know—with help."

"A school for engineers—in Aldestow?" The concept was intriguing. If there was a school right in town—right up the hill—then maybe Lewis wouldn't be the only one. . . . "What sort of help?"

"Well, you, to start with," she said directly.

to see it once. That's more than most folks get."

More than your father, even, he didn't say—
but she heard the unspoken words.

"Papa didn't need to see the Phoenix to
believe in it," she said, chin lifting. "He knew—he
understood—before any of us. *Credendo vides.*
'By believing, one sees.'"

"Yeah." She was right. It was amazing
what you could see once you believed. Once
you believed in *yourself.* "Come on. I'm gettin'
hungry. Let's go see what Sebastian has in the
galley."

Together, they walked back across the deck
of the *Basset*—and into their future.

A NOTE FROM THE AUTHOR

Fire Bird begins in Cornwall, the southernmost peninsula of Great Britain and something of a "land of legend" in its own right. There is no Cornish town called Aldestow, but alert readers who know Cornwall may notice some striking similarities between my invented village and the seacoast town of Padstow, with its treacherous, mermaid-cursed harbor. Alert readers who don't know Cornwall (or who would like to know more) can investigate Cornish history and folklore in Claude Berry's loving description of his homeland, *Portrait of Cornwall*.

The Basilisk, the Phoenix, and the salamander are all creatures steeped in centuries of mythological tradition. The legend of the Phoenix, for example, extends all the way back to ancient Egypt, where the Phoenix itself may well be associated with yet another remarkable bird, the Benu—the purple heron held sacred to the sun in the city of Heliopolis. Readers interested in fantastical beasts could do worse than to check out *Bulfinch's Mythology, Volume I: The Age of Fable.* (This classic work is also available online in an annotated and hyperlinked text at www.bulfinch.org.) In addition, T. H. White's translation of a twelfth-century medieval bestiary, *The Book of Beasts,* contains much interesting Phoenix lore (not to mention salamander and Basilisk lore), as does Peter Lum's wider survey of the creatures of world mythology, *Fabulous Beasts.*

James Alexander, the lighthouse engineer, and Lewis Trelawny, his apprentice, are of course fictional characters, but the lighthouse of Alexandria—the Pharos—was an actual place. Built not long after 300 B.C. by Sostratus of Cnidus, it was one of the Seven Wonders of the Ancient World, faithfully lighting the night for sailors until it was destroyed by an earthquake sometime during the thirteenth century. I make no apologies for moving the Pharos into the Lands of Legend; it belongs there. For those readers who want to learn more about actual lighthouses, I recommend *A History of Lighthouses* by Patrick Beaver. For those more intrigued by the builders than by the buildings, I suggest Bella Bathurst's *The Lighthouse Stevensons,* about the fabulous Stevenson family of Scotland—including, incidentally, a grandson, one Robert Louis Stevenson, who rejected engineering in favor of a career as (gasp!) a novelist.

In fact, I think it might be appropriate to let the author of such tales as *Kidnapped* and *Treasure Island* have the last word here. "When I smell salt water," wrote Robert Louis Stevenson proudly in 1880, "I know that I am not far from the works of my ancestors." And again, in 1886: "[My father], two of my uncles, my grandfather, and my great grandfather in succession, have been engineers to the Scotch Lighthouse service; all the sea lights in Scotland are signed with our name; and my father's services to lighthouse optics have been distinguished indeed. I might write books till 1900 and not serve humanity so well."

ABOUT THE AUTHOR

A lifelong resident of Oak Park, Illinois, MARY FRANCES ZAMBRENO has always been fascinated by lighthouses—and by phoenixes. She decided to become a writer at the age of twelve, when she first realized that writers were just people with a good supply of paper and a desire to tell stories. Along the way to becoming a writer, she earned a doctorate in medieval literature, learned to read six languages (including English), and discovered that she enjoyed teaching almost as much as she enjoyed writing. Currently, she teaches at a college in the Chicago area and continues to work at becoming a writer. Her young adult fantasy novel *A Plague of Sorcerers* was named to the ALA's list of Best Books for Young Adults in 1992; its sequel, *Journeyman Wizard,* was a New York Public Library Book for the Teen Age in 1994.

Books by Tamora Pierce
THE SONG OF THE LIONESS QUARTET
Alanna: The First Adventure
In the Hand of the Goddess
The Woman Who Rides Like a Man
Lioness Rampant

THE IMMORTALS QUARTET
Wild Magic
Wolf-Speaker
Emperor Mage
The Realms of the Gods

PROTECTOR OF THE SMALL
First Test
Page
Squire

Books by Carol Hughes
Toots and the Upside-Down House
Jack Black and the Ship of Thieves
    AND COMING SOON
Toots Underground